David Leonard

Westward Bound, Alone

iUniverse, Inc.
Bloomington

Westward Bound, Alone

iUniverse books may be ordered through booksellers or by contacting:

iUniverse
1663 Liberty Drive
Bloomington, IN 47403
www.iuniverse.com
1-800-Authors (1-800-288-4677)

ISBN: 978-1-4759-4430-3 (sc)
ISBN: 978-1-4759-4431-0 (ebk)

Library of Congress Control Number: 2012914549

Printed in the United States of America

iUniverse rev. date: 08/17/2012

Chapter 1

Wagons

He'd been eating dust behind the wagons. The dust was a ground cloud, blinding everyone four or five wagons rearward from the lead. The outriders were blessed with the absence of dust, but this was needful, as they were out there to give warning of war parties and act as guides. They led the wagons through the rough land and, they hoped, to water. With no breeze, the dust was held close to the ground round the forty-odd wagons—or, at least, those behind the front few.

Dan was brooding about his real parents. They were dead and gone, but they'd always be in Dan's memory. Pa had taught Dan that family was everything. Ma and Pa could be turned to anytime. It'd always been that way. Then they'd died. And he'd had to say a final good-bye to his sister, Sarah. He hated change.

It was past noon as the wagons bumped through the sagebrush. Josh and Mary's wagon was bringing up the rear of the train, so they were totally blind, but, as for that, most of the train was as blinded in the dust.

This delay in the noon break might be hinting of something good coming. Or it might just be the captain of the train wanting to push on. He'd do that sometimes just to show who was boss, Dan knew.

Dan Fitzgerald was either fourteen or fifteen. He wasn't positive but thought he might be fifteen. His black hair was in need of cutting. His eyes were sky-blue, and his face was tanned. It was a strong face, unlined for all he'd been through. He'd been thin before the wagons started and was thinner now. He was strong—near as strong as some men he knew. But he stuttered. And he'd found that some folks thought stuttering meant you were slow and dumb.

Dan was scared when Ma and Pa died. Shortly before he breathed his last, Pa had put his arm around both Sarah and himself and said, "Never give up. Life ain't always a fair thing. Jest keep goin'."

Dan just couldn't believe they were gone. Gone. It'd happened so quick. And life changed forever for Sarah and him. Josh and Mary asked the two if they would like to live with them. Mary had said, "Think about it, and let us know what you decide. We'd like to have you."

Later, in the old cabin, Sarah asked Dan what he thought. They knew the Martins. The folks had become friends with them in the small church congregation where they'd gone to worship.

Dan was the very end-most part of the train; he trod close to the tailgate of the Martins' wagon. Tomorrow they'd go up to lead wagon.

Dan traveled with the Martin wagon because he and Sarah had long ago agreed that going to live with Mary and Josh was the thing to do. Really, there'd been little choice. Dan was only about nine and Sarah fourteen. Going on alone in the old cabin would have been miserable, if not impossible.

Ma and Pa had been "hardscrabble" farmers who had only a small corn patch. Pa had brought in wild game for the table.

He worked for others when he could. They'd scratched out an existence with Dan helping out. He'd only a few years of schoolin'. Dan knew he couldn't make any sort a livin'—not for himself *and* Sarah. They'd go with the Martins and see how it was.

Sarah was soon under Mary's wing, and they'd become close friends. Colleen had looked up to Sarah like an older sister. Josh had just treated Dan like a man. Dan knew that Josh and Mary liked him even with the stutter and poor talking. They weren't his real parents, but they tried. They'd opened their home and hearts to the orphans. They'd sent Dan to the little school down by the church. Maybe they wouldn't if they had known what torture it was for Dan and his stutter.

He had more than a few fights because of the stutter. Some of the older boys tried him out but found they'd tackled a bear-cat. He'd hit the first bully a fair lick and got blooded a bit in return. Still, the boy was big and knew he been fetched a dandy hit or two. Soon, he didn't want any more. It'd been that way with a few more of the bigger boys with about the same results. Dan was a boy to stay away from, and most did.

Josh didn't try to boss him. He left Dan lots of room. In turn, he'd grown to like Josh. He looked up to him. Josh always told him the truth about things but didn't preach at him. He'd known about the fights and just told Dan not to take any abusin'. "Fight, and if it's unfair, tell me" was all Josh said. Josh was a quiet man with a ready smile.

In less than a year, Dan was callin' Mary and Josh "Ma and Pa." It just came natural. Mary and Josh held hands with Sarah, Dan, and Colleen every morning at prayer. Why this was important Dan couldn't say. It seemed, though, to crowd out that awful feelin' he'd had when they'd buried his Ma and Pa. That was when the stutter started. Holdin' hands was new and, somehow, special; it made him feel *needed.*

3

Mary wasn't his real mother, but he was drawn to her. She clearly held out a warm heart to this lonely boy with the stutter. It was something he needed more than he knew.

Sarah had married Moses shortly before the Martins sold out to join the wagons bound for the Oregon Country. It was a sad parting for Dan and Sarah.

Sarah approached him and said, "Dan, Moses and I will stay to farm with his Pa on halves. We won't be going to Oregon."

"W . . . w . . . we won't s . . . s . . . see you a . . . a . . . any mo . . . mo . . . more, ever!" Dan said.

"Oh! Dan, there'll surely be mail before too long. Then we'll write to each other," Sarah said. She stepped close and put an arm around him.

"No, we'll nev . . . nev . . . never s . . . s . . . see you again!"

Dan had his head down, and Sarah was afraid for him. She couldn't think of what to say. She hugged him and found herself crying. Separating was a tough thing.

"Fir . . . fir . . . first it wa . . . wa . . . was Ma an . . . an . . . and Pa . . ."

Sarah understood. Parting was crushing Daniel. And she knew she couldn't help him.

Sarah's adopted family felt deep sadness, too. Likely, they'd not see one another for the rest of their lives. But Dan had no desire to remain behind in Missouri. He'd caught the Oregon fever from Josh. Besides, he didn't want to be separated from Colleen. She was special to Dan. She never seemed to notice the stutter. He badly needed a friend, and Colleen was a friend.

She was, maybe, a bit younger than Dan. She was golden-haired and seemed fond of Dan's company. She chose mostly to be with him by the wagon as they walked west.

Today, though, Colleen was keeping as much out of the dust as she could get by staying inside the wagon with her Ma. Canvas was drawn behind the front bench and closed down over the tailgate. It made for warm travel but was likely better than the terrible cloud of dirt.

Colleen was more than just pretty. She'd always done little things for Sarah and Dan. She was the most thoughtful person he'd ever met. She was a quiet girl who was kind to any animal or person in need. She never seemed to think of herself first. Dan was deeply affected by the goodness he saw in both Colleen and her Ma.

Ma seldom corrected or scolded Dan. He'd come to be her special project. Aside from correcting his poor talk from time to time, she mostly worried about the stutter. She knew when it'd started and fretted about what to do. And she knew he was too solitary. Often, he'd wander off to hunt or just be by himself. She knew he brooded about things too much.

Josh shared Mary's worry about Dan. He remembered the days before Dan's parents had died. "Shock" was Josh's estimate of why Dan stuttered.

Mary thought about it and said, "I'm not sure. And he goes off by himself so much."

Colleen had overheard the discussion and said, "I think he can't stand *parting*. His parents dying was a terrible and final parting, and now it's Sarah. That's probably near final, too."

Though he didn't know it, Dan was handsome. Even now, he showed signs of becoming a striking man. His chin was square below a high-ridged nose and a full mouth. He already had broad shoulders even as he topped out at just over five feet.

Suddenly, the wagon pulled off and stopped by the wagon in front. Great! Time for food and a break from the awful dust! Dan was ready for some food. As he walked around the wagon, he could see the tops of cottonwood trees. This surely meant water! Josh was already walking ahead and hollered back at Dan to unhitch the team. Dan liked it that Josh treated him as a grown man, and he quickly started unhitching the team from the wagon tongue and single trees.

Soon it was possible to see youngsters running off to the right of the teams and dropping out of sight down an incline. Another sure sign of water! Mary and Colleen had removed cooking pots from the wagon and had walked ahead to join the wagons in front, where there'd likely be a feed of biscuits and antelope meat. *The women work even harder than the men,* Dan thought. Soon they'd be busy washin' clothes, he knew.

Before long, Josh appeared and started unbuckling the harness on the sorrel. Dan quickly unbuckled the straps from the collar of the dun. He knew Josh would tell him what was happenin' in his own time.

They slapped the harness over the wagon tongue and started walking the horses past the wagons lined up ahead. They were behind several teams being led to water.

"Water," Josh said, "and good runnin' water."

Dan was as short-winded as his Pa and just nodded. Soon they saw the creek. Then they saw that the small stream was turning off sharply to the south away from the wagons. They'd hit the steam right at a bend as the water began flowing south. Some wagons had crossed. *With luck, we might move ahead alongside the runnin' water,* Dan thought.

Young boys were already tending teams as they pranced in the small stream. Nearby, off to the north, Dan noticed a cliff on the side of a hill facing the train. He thought, maybe, he'd like to go up there.

"Wo . . . wo . . . wonder how long we . . . we . . . we'll be camped," he said to no one.

Mary and the women served up broth—it was hot but good in spite of the heat of the day.

Dan was handed a bowl, a biscuit, and a tin of tea. He moved under the shade of the nearest cottonwood sittin' cross-legged on the ground near Josh and the other men. They wolfed down the food in silence. Dan knew he'd soon be takin' a turn mindin' the horses.

He was resting on his back, sleepily listening when Ike started to say something. Then a horseman came up. Dan opened his eyes and saw the train's captain looking around the group.

"Well, boys, this water don't trail with us fer much. We'll camp a bit."

"How long do you think?" asked one of the men.

The captain spat and said, "Can't say fer certain. Kinkaid says the stream turns out to the north in a few miles, and we'll need to rest the teams for the dry road ahead. Need to start fillin' barrels again."

Dan idly wondered what he meant by *road*. But a rest would be good.

"Well," said Ike, "it looks like rain before long. It's as good we stay planted for a day or two."

Before he knew what was happening, Josh shook his arm and he was awake. He arose and walked to the wagon to collect the old musket. He made sure the gun was loaded, fetched his possibles bag, and was movin' off to take his shift with the stock. The teams were herded together, separate from the cattle. They would be moved from time to time to new grass alongside the water.

Dan knew it was an important duty. You had to keep a careful eye out for Indians, and he could very well fail to see any until it was too late. If he saw any, he'd fire the old musket in warnin'.

Today, they'd fetch the horses back to the wagons come evening and move the wagons into a circle. They had to leave the stock outside the wagons in order to graze, which meant that armed guards were necessary out with the herds. The small bunch of cattle numbered only twenty head, but the horses numbered over a hundred head.

Sometime that night, a rain started up. Dan moved to the Murphy's wagon and crawled under for shelter. Colleen was camped with her Ma and Pa under their wagon. No campfires tonight.

Chapter 2

The Hill

In early morning, they ate a breakfast of antelope meat, biscuits, and tea. The rain was not a heavy downfall, but it'd soon be coming by the looks of it. Dan would be out to get his share of herding later in the day. Now he felt refreshed and restless.

He saw some boys pounding stakes into the ground for pitching horseshoes. *About as excitin' as watchin' an old cow chew her cud*, Dan thought.

After Josh had gone off to see someone, Dan walked up to the wagon where Mary and Colleen sat in out of the slow drizzle. He got the old musket and his buckskin jacket.

"Where are you off to, Dan?" asked Mary.

"O . . . o . . . oh, I th . . . th . . . thought I might g . . . g . . . go over on th . . . th . . . that hill and see what I mi . . . mi . . . might."

Mary said, "Now, Daniel, you take some food with you."

Dan was impatient to be off and very nearly refused the jerky and biscuits that she handed him. Shrugging, he stuffed them into his possibles bag and hurried off.

Colleen had been watching Dan as if waiting for an invitation to join him.

He wouldn't mind having Colleen coming but, for some reason, just didn't want company this morning.

He seemed to seek solitude too much. It was a feature of his that worried Mary. And that stutter had only begun when his parents died. What caused it? Maybe Josh was right. Maybe it was shock. Then, again, she thought that Colleen was nearer to the truth. Partings did cause Dan to suffer. She'd thought much about what she might do but felt helpless.

He'd climbed halfway up the hill, which was steeper than he'd thought. It was getting slippery from the rain. More than once, he caught himself before he fell. He paused near the top as the rain came harder. He'd like to find shelter where he might rest and eat a bit of the jerky. He wished he'd left the musket back in the wagon. It was a handful with trying to climb the muddy hill.

His thoughts went back to the old mountain man who'd appeared at their campfire one evening at what the grizzled old fellow had called "The Divide." It had been cool that evening, and Dan heard Ma and Pa wondering why. It wasn't the time of year to be that cool. But their curiosity was soon answered as Moss, as he called himself, explained. They were camped on the "easy passage o'er the divide whence water either flowed east to the Atlantic Ocean or west to the Pacific." It was hard to believe. It was about 7,000 feet high on the Devide. They didn't feel like they'd climbed that much but knew that the big Shining Mountains were visible a bit to the south and east. Moss had called this the "South Pass." Hot in the day and cool at night. That had been several weeks earlier. Dan missed old Moss. He'd become a friend. Maybe it was best to not have a friendship. It'd never last.

His appearance got everyone's attention. They'd stared at him. He seemed not to notice. His old buckskins were black from grease and blood and fires. He looked like something wild and more than a little uncivilized. His gray hair hung below his shoulders.

Moss was only a few inches shy of six feet. His face was covered with gray whiskers that hung nearly to his waist. His face, though, seemed humorous under a coonskin cap. His old buckskin outfit sported a few remaining strands of buckskin that were snipped off for every kind of need.

His boots were knee high and formed his primary decoration. They showed colorful beads and porcupine needles. Best, they were fur-lined for winter cold. He'd worn them in the evening maybe to show 'em off. But in the warm weather, he wore moccasins.

It was kind of hard to tell how old Moss might be, but Dan thought that "old" fit the bill pretty well. Moss might be in his late forties or late sixties. It was hard to tell. Moss was happy, and it showed from every pore. He just didn't waste time brooding. His smiling brown eyes were set in a round face over a broad nose.

Dan had been daydreaming and glanced behind him. He could barely see the wagons though the heavy rain. He wondered how far he'd walked. He knew that distances would fool a person in this western country. He'd traveled a lot farther than he'd thought it would be. He'd started out an hour before and knew he'd soon be tuckered with all this slip-slidin' in the mud.

When he got back, he'd probably be late for his turn at herdin'. Josh would be a bit upset, he knew, though his pa was seldom overly critical. He expected Dan to learn things through tryin'. Josh was patient with him, and he treated Dan like his own son. He'd been that way since Dan's parents were buried back in Missouri. Like Ma, Josh just didn't hear his stutter.

Not watching where he stepped in the wet mud, he suddenly felt his feet go out from under, and he began a fast slide. *Damn.*

Chapter 3

Darkness

H e shifted, not comfortable, and opened his eyes. There was total darkness. It was like his nightmare of bein' in a grave. It was darker than a night without a moon. *Maybe I'm under the wagon,* he thought. His head ached terribly, and his right hip hurt. Thinking it curious he didn't hear any camp noises, he drifted off into a dreamless sleep.

Later, he awakened and, again, wondered if he was under a wagon. There were no stars—*maybe it was the clouds*—and it surely was cold. There were none of the usual camp noises. Something was bad wrong.

The ground under him was completely dry! Where was the rain? Then it came with a rush—the hillside, the slide down to nothin'. Where was he? Had he fallen or slid into a hole? Had this just happened? How long had he been here? He felt the pain on his right side and decided to try standin'. So far, so good. Sore, but he didn't think he'd broken a bone. His head hurt, and he felt a large bump under his hair. *Oh, Lord!* Where was his hat? And the musket! And it was cold as hell! His possibles bag still hung from his shoulder

A thought came unbidden—was this a snake den? He didn't hear a thing. He could stand and cautiously shuffled around in the cold dark with his feet, trying to feel for the musket. Finally, tired, confused, and still fearful of snakes in the dark, he dropped to his hands and knees and started crawling in circles.

He was near giving up when his hand touched the cool metal of the old flintlock. He felt carefully along the lock and was relieved that the flint was still in place. Then his hand touched the old slouch hat under the stock. His hand slid to his side where he kept his skinning knife. It was still there.

The darkness was total. He had no idea which way to turn. Slowly he began taking small steps. Where was he! He soon decided he was moving a bit downward, though it might be his imagination. How could he ever get out of this absolute darkness? He took several abrupt tumbles over rocks before returning to his hands and knees to crawl again. After what seemed forever on his hands and knees, he became aware of a noise. It was water!

What if he fell into a pool of water down here? He was blind and, besides, he couldn't swim a lick. The thought chilled him, and he was plenty cold as it was. What a way to die. In a deep pool, in total, cold darkness! He wouldn't even know which way to go to reach the side of a pool . . . even if he could swim. It was getting louder as he inched farther down the incline.

Then his hand felt nothing! He was on the edge of somethin' . . . maybe a high cliff. He could hear water runnin' somewhere far below. Pushing backward, he knew a bone-jarring panic. Should he turn around and move up the incline?

He moved carefully to his left, feeling his way inch by inch. After moving what seemed several yards, his hand came in contact with rock on his left side. Exploring as best he could in the darkness, he began to think he'd found a rock wall. Maybe he'd found the side of whatever this was. What now?

Go back? He doubted that he even knew what *back* meant. Would he be able to retrace his steps?

After a moment of despair, he moved slowly to what he thought was forward, huggin' the rock he felt on the left. In an hour or so—how to know how much time had passed?—the sound of the water was comin' dimmer. Had he really passed that danger? He knew he had a fear of the water. Maybe it was farther down in some crack, posin' an even greater danger?

He was exhausted. He knew he couldn't have come any great distance from where he'd woken up. And he was hungry and cold. Ironically, he craved a drink of cold water. He felt in his possibles bag and fingered the meager supply of jerky he'd so carelessly taken at Mary's insistence. Why hadn't he brought more biscuits! He put one small piece of jerky in his mouth, sucking slowly.

He lay in the cold darkness and closed his eyes. He dreamed of seein' Pa and Ma in their coffins; he hated that frequent nightmare. It had been a scary thing to see them totally still and dead. He thought a dead person was like someone *judgin'*, somehow. They let you condemn yourself. *Why were they dead and not me?*

It was the first time he'd been to a funeral that he could remember. The bodies had been laid out in the cabin before bein' put into their rude boxes. It made him sick to see the ropes lower the bodies into the ground and to hear the clods hittin' the tops of the coffins. He hated the dream. Nothin' was as final as death.

He awoke with a jerk, again half lost in sleep. Where was he! How long had he slept? Nothin' made sense. Which direction had he been goin'? He pulled the musket close and began crawling until his left hand again came against rock. Cautiously rising, he felt the rock extend high overhead. He was sure it formed some kind of wall. He went back to his knees and back to crawling.

He could barely hear the water and soon lost all sound of it. He was still on what seemed to be a downward incline covered with rocks and boulders. Well, come to that, wasn't an incline always *down*? He grinned in the darkness and wondered if he'd ever get out. He would refuse to deal with the tight fear he knew was in his belly. It was just so totally dark and cold!

Then he had a terrible thought. *How long would the wagons wait?* Were they out lookin' for him? Surely Ma and Pa and Colleen would be lookin' for him. He knew he had to get out of the crazy darkness! The wagons couldn't wait long for him to show up. A few days' delay was serious; fall was comin', and snow could soon be a big problem. He wanted to stand and run but knew this was simple panic with nothin' to gain but a bad fall and the possible loss of the musket. No. He had to stop. Think this through. Go forward, or what he thought was *forward*, or try to retrace his steps. After all, he'd entered the darkness somewhere very close to where he'd woken up.

His thoughts quickly assured him he could not retrace his steps in the utter darkness. Besides, he'd surely fallen some distance and been knocked unconscious. No, somehow he couldn't convince himself that going back was the thing to try. He did not know where he'd started out from anyhow.

His mind turned to the old mountain man who'd appeared at their campfire. He'd made himself comfortable and given Mary a "thank ye" when she'd handed him a biscuit and a tin of hot tea. When he'd devoured the biscuit without a fare-ye-well or whatever, darned if she'd not given him another! Josh had grinned and asked where the old man was headed.

"I call myself 'Moss,' and a rollin' stone'll get none. Not right sure where I'm headin'. Maybe north. Not right sure."

Old Moss was irresistible. You had to like the old fellow. There was no pretense in Moss. And he either liked you or he didn't. For some reason, he'd liked the Martins. He'd stayed only two days with the wagon before riding off after tea one morning. They'd not seen him again. Dan had brooded and said hardly a word to anyone for several days.

Some of the things old Moss had said came to mind in the cold darkness. He'd told them about the days when he'd trapped for beaver in the cold western waters. He and his fellow trappers had spent winters in camp or, maybe a time or two, with an Indian tribe.

"Surviven were keeping yer eyes open and yer powder dry. Ya learn quick to sleep with one eye open if'en ya wants to keep yer topnotch. An' ya be real careful whar ya sets yer fire. Keep it real small. Build it under a tree so's the smoke gets thinned, and use dry wood. Go to sleep somewheres out of sight and go with naught a fire at night. Better be cold then wakin' up with an injun drivin' a knife into yer gizzard. An keep a eye on yer hoss. He'll save ya from some bad surprises. He smells things ya don't, and his ears talk to ya. Ya just got to learn how to listen. Say, don't cotton to bright trinkets on yer gear. The sun can get ya in real bad if'en ya wear bright doodads."

He'd talked like he was near starved to talk. He'd talked with Dan and Colleen about the things he'd learned in his years in the West. He loved it. He'd talked to them about such things, and more, as they'd walked along by the wagon, his horse, Max, trailing like a dog. He'd talked of so many things. Things Dan hadn't thought of. He'd said you needed to travel quiet. "Keep things in your gear so'n they don't jingle." He'd given Dan a cheerful and interesting schoolin' though Dan had never thought of it as "schoolin'" till much later. He liked old Moss and knew that Moss liked Colleen and him. He was a bit shy around Colleen, but they were comfortable together. And, like his family, Moss seemed not to notice his stutter.

Dan opened his eyes to the darkness and thought and thought *hard*. Old Moss would know what to do. He'd love to have the old man by his side right then. He knew that Moss would never consider it impossible. He'd always think it through.

Again, Dan wondered if there wasn't something he could do. Could he get a fire goin' to see and get his bearin's? No. No fuel in this cold, rocky cavern. Then he thought he felt a tiny breeze touch his face. Or was he just wishful thinkin' again?

He knew he was tirin' and his mind was wanderin'. How long had he been crawlin'? He didn't know. Had he been down here two days? Longer? How long had he slept after he fell? There was no answer.

He dropped his head on his arms and slept.

Chapter 4

Light!

H e opened his eyes to a bad pain in his head and glared into the darkness. Again, he wondered how much time had passed. Was it day or night? Maybe he'd only been awake at night. Maybe some light would come when it was daytime. This seemed unlikely, he knew.

He reached into his possibles bag and fingered the last piece of jerky. Then, before he could argue himself out of it, he had it in his mouth. He sucked greedily at the small piece of dried meat. Oh, for a drink of water!

"Hell," he muttered, "time to quit wishin' and time to get movin'. Don't quit."

Putting action to words, he pushed himself forward, bumping into rocks and the rough wall. He felt he had to move more to the right or what seemed to be right, but it was hard to tell with the climbing over and around large boulders. His knees and shoulders were sore from bumping into rocks. And his head hurt like hell. The thirst was terrible. Then he recalled Moss saying something about suckin' on a pebble to help with thirst. He found a tiny stone and, sure enough, it helped!

He slowly began to feel something else. A faint breath of cool air was touching his face! How long since his fall into this nightmare? *What if the wagons had gone on?* These thoughts brought an added urgency. Then he stopped and closed his eyes, holding his painful head.

No. Got to use my head. Can't go off half-cock.

He tried to find the jagged stone wall he'd been following. Nothing but rubble and boulders. So easy to get turned round and get confused. So twisted he had no idea where he was going without the wall, and that was pretty dubious. He stayed put, trying to figure it out. Then it came to him.

He licked his finger and held it over his head. Yes! The cool air dried his finger slightly on the right side. He had a guide! Maybe.

Moving on in a crawl, he felt something bump him painfully on his head and rub against his back. The top would no longer allow for crawlin' on hands and knees. Had he come this far only to be trapped? He felt squeezed between tons of rock and became sick to his stomach. It was his worst moment since wakin'. After moving slowly toward the fresh air on his stomach—and every few seconds assurin' himself that he was going toward it—he soon realized he had moved into some large space. He could not explain it, but he *felt* it. Could there be some tiny amount of light that made him so sure that he was in a very large place?

Got to move.

Cautiously standing, he reached over his head and could touch nothing. He tried to ease his sore back as he stood, stretching and bending over. He stretched and bent at the waist several times. It felt better! Oh, to be able to walk like a man again! And to gaze overhead at stars and the moon! What great friends they were. Now he was dizzy.

He returned to his crawling to avoid his constant falling and sank down to his belly to rest for just a minute. He had a troubled sleep filled with terrible dreams. He was trying to keep up with the Martin wagon but was unable and chased them in darkness. He jerked himself awake.

How long had he slept this time? Was there something wrong? Was he sick? Why couldn't he stay awake? Shrugging his shoulders, he again checked for the fresh air and followed his wet finger. Soon, the current of warmer air was strong enough that he no longer had to check with his finger. And he was convinced that there was a faint light. That must mean it was daytime, or maybe a bright moon, but certainly some kind of openin' ahead!

The faint light was soon strong enough for him to see a bit of his surroundings. He reached out to grab an overhead rock. It broke, leaving a small stone in his hand. It felt heavy and, not thinking about it, he stuck it in his jacket pocket.

He was now able to move mostly on his feet. After hours of groping around what he thought was going to be an endless outgrowth of rock, he found himself suddenly in what seemed the strongest light he'd ever seen. He blinked and closed his eyes; he'd been in darkness so long that his eyes had to get used to light. Fighting the glare, he realized that a long slit seemed to run between two or three feet high over a few dozen feet long. It was high up, and he couldn't see much else because there was too much light!

He worked his way toward the light, still carrying the old musket. He dared not return without that musket! Josh would be upset if that was gone. As it was, he knew he'd probably not be a welcome sight after the long delay for Josh's wagon—or maybe worse. His haste to return became slowed with misgivings. How much trouble was he in?

When he'd moved forward and under the opening, he found a welcome sight: loose rock like a staircase led to a long flat opening. But it soon proved to be a last and serious hurdle. The loose rock began sliding down as soon as he tried to climb. With escape from his entrapment so close, it began to enrage Dan. He rushed at the rock and slid backward at each attempt to climb.

So close! Damn! And damn again.

Finally, exhausted, he sat and stared at the slide area. Slowly his anger subsided, and he studied the slide. Far to the right, he thought he could see some larger rocks that might afford some kind of foothold. If he could get high enough, he might be able to get a hand on the rocks overhead.

Well, it's got to be done, he thought. *Rest. Don't rush this time. Go slow and sure.* This might be the only chance he'd have to get out of this underground hell.

He awoke with a start. Slept again! What was happenin'? He knew it might be lack of water—or something worse. He had a terrible thirst! The pebble no longer helped. His head still hurt. He felt the large bump just above his ear. The bump was smaller now. How could he get out in this shape? Trembles shook his arms and legs. Well, it was there to be done.

He worked his way through the rocks at the bottom of the slide until he reached his planned route. Testing each rock, he began climbing. He thought it could only be fifteen feet or so to the opening. It was so close and so frustrating.

Finally, he reached the spot he knew would force him to go slow and careful. One false step and he'd be right back where he started. He reached out and got a hand on a jagged rock overhead. Would it hold? Slowly he pulled himself upward and pushed with the one toehold he'd found. Just inches to go. He caught sight of a beautiful blue sky. The sun must have sunk toward the horizon so he could see without the glare. His eyes were becoming more used to the light. He moved his hand up and found the second jagged rock that held as he pulled himself up. He pushed his body through the narrow opening. He was out!

Had they even looked in this openin'? As he stood, he saw it was hidden pretty well by brush.

He tried to run and tumbled several feet down the steep hillside. He caught himself in the tall brush and knew he had to go slow. This would be a great time to break a leg . . . or the old flintlock.

As he rounded the hillside, he saw the tops of the cottonwoods. He moved as fast as possible and saw only trees. The wagons were gone.

Chapter 5

Campsite

His first need was an absolute—*water*. He fell down at the stream, ducking his head and drinking the cold, wonderful water. He'd heard a terrible thirst should be doctored with care—you ought to drink slowly and not overdo it—but he drank till his thirst was slaked.

He walked through the shallow stream and gazed at the spot where the wagons had stood. How long had they waited? The tracks were faint. Maybe weather had done this. Wind, he knew, could cover tracks fast with sand. And there had been heavy rain the day he'd gone. He was in shock. How long since they'd left? How long had they looked? The worst thing was that it was his fault.

Totally done in, he dropped to the ground and gazed at the sky from under the cottonwood where he'd eaten with Josh and Ike. That had been the first shade they'd found for several dusty miles. When had that been? Surely not that much time had gone by! Lord! What to do now? He was starvin' and probably sicker than he knew.

Flat on his back, he studied the tops of the trees. Maybe? No. Climbin' the trees would reveal nothin' of the wagons. Hilly country was ahead, accordin' to the outriders. If they'd made good time, they'd be forty or fifty miles away! Could that be? He was dazed, knowin' he'd not catch up with the wagons. Worse, he'd have to stick to the stream, which would soon turn north while the wagons would veer off to the west. He had become seriously depressed and angered. And he had no one to blame but himself.

Something distracted him in the swaying tree branches. He noted it like he would a fly buzzing about. Abruptly he sat up. He was catchin' sight of something that shouldn't be there. He walked closer and saw a leather bag hangin' high off the ground.

His heart was beating fast. Maybe they'd not just left him! He quickly caught a low branch and climbed to the swinging bag. He soon had the leather strap untied and dropped to the ground. It felt heavy. He opened the bag and had an instant of intense longing to see Josh, Mary, and Colleen. They'd not just deserted him!

He pulled out about three pounds of jerked meat. Next came several dried biscuits. He had a piece of jerky in his mouth and quickly chewed. It was the best thing he'd had since . . . *then*. He stuffed a biscuit in his mouth and made for the stream. Drinking fast, he managed to swallow and felt tears come to his eyes. They'd remembered him! He felt ashamed that he'd allowed himself to think the worst of Ma and Pa.

He turned to see what else was in the bag. Nearly half a pound of black power in a small leather bag. Then, folded neat near the bottom, was Colleen's greatest treasure. It was her colored cotton scarf. He felt tears come to his eyes. As he pulled it from the bag, he knew something was inside the scarf. Folded in paper were a dozen lead balls for the musket.

When he unfolded the paper, he saw it was a page from Mary's old Bible—the page where family names were added with the dates of births. He saw Colleen's name and birthday followed by his sister, Sarah, and the date of her coming to live with Josh and Mary . . . as if it were her birthday. Then came his name and the same date as his sister. He'd not seen this before and felt a lump come in his throat. He quickly blinked away tears and found the last two items in the treasure bag. There was an extra flint for the musket and a small firebox made of tin with dry moss inside. They'd thought of it all!

At that moment, he knew he'd find them—no matter how long it took. He'd find them . . . if he lived.

He held the scarf against his cheek. Colleen had given . . . all of them had given the best they could. That moment he knew a full heart. As he began to carefully refold the page from the Bible, he saw a faint printing on the backside. He could just make out the words.

> *Dan son luked for ye for 2 day. hostls showd. figered they gotten ye had to moov on. if'n you gat th—stickk to the water. prayin you gat th-s Pa*

He stared into space, fully realizin' he was alone. *No chance in hell of catchin' up afoot. No way at all.* Lying back in the bright afternoon, he shut his eyes.

When he opened his eyes, the sun was just moving down and out of sight. He was shocked. How could he just fall asleep like that! How sick was he? What if those Indians had come back! It was comin' dark, and he'd not found a safe place to bed down. He had to start thinkin'!

Soon he'd found a depression behind a large cottonwood near the willows and the stream. He looked to the musket. Flint was in place, so he tapped the barrel down on a rock. He saw a small glob of dirt fall out. He knew he'd missed a bad blowup if he'd fired the gun. An old smooth bore and not terribly accurate, but it was what he had!

He took off his buckskin jacket and carefully laid out all that he had from his possibles bag and the treasure bag. Fifteen balls and maybe half a pound of black powder. A guess was three pounds of jerked meat, and there were four dried biscuits. He had an extra flint for the musket and a firebox with dry moss. And he had the musket and his knife. He picked up the scarf and peered long at it in the half light. Next he placed the page from the Bible down.

He knew he had to think every step through if he wanted to stay alive. According to Moss, there were lots of ways to die. He'd said that if the Indians didn't get you, the freezin' colds of winter would work, or a broken leg, or snakebite, or a dozen other things.

He carefully packed the treasure bag with food and hung it from a high branch, trying to hide it high against the tree where it might not be seen or reached by wolves or coyotes. But he doubted they'd come near his human smell. His possibles bag would carry his ball and powder, flint and firebox. And Colleen's scarf. Someday he'd return it.

The old flintlock was a worry. How could he prime the pan quickly? Hating to do it, he fetched the page from the Bible. He tore small pieces from it and wrapped a pinch of black power in each small paper.

"Well, they're my powder pills," he muttered as he stuffed them into the pocket of his jacket. He would be able to break a paper and fill the pan quickly. Still, it would be only one shot at a time.

Finally, he searched the land in all directions. Nothin'. No campfires. Just . . . nothin'.

He looked up at the stars that were beginning to fill the night sky. "Never knew how much I missed ya before."

Then his eyes fluttered shut, and he slept.

Chapter 6

Moving On

When Dan next opened his eyes, he knew it was before dawn. Rising, he shook his stiff frame and drank deeply at the stream. Then he fetched the bag from the high tree branch.

"Follow the wagons," he whispered.

For how long? He remembered an outrider saying they'd soon leave the stream, which was turning northward. The wagons were to hold due west. If he left the stream, how would he carry water without a skin? Josh was right. Follow the stream. Without water, he'd surely die. He wondered why Josh hadn't thought to leave him a water skin—maybe to take away any temptation to follow the wagons. He'd never be able to carry enough water for a long walk into arid country. Pa had been thinkin' real careful. The wagons would have a time of it—even with the barrels of water.

He tried not to think about how impossible it would be to catch up with the wagons. Instead, he walked to the stream and drank again before attaching the treasure bag to his possibles bag. He lifted the musket. He was hungry but was afraid of eating from his small stock of food. Time to move. He felt like crying. He had never felt so alone.

He recalled old Moss sayin' how you never start the day without checkin' your gun. He felt the flint and pan. He stood the musket on end and peered down the barrel. It'd be a miracle if he'd gotten rid of all the dirt. He tapped the muzzle against a rock, but no more dirt turned out. Then he put the ramrod into the muzzle and pushed it down to where it seemed to reach the ball. Satisfied, he put the ramrod back in its holders under the barrel.

He wheeled his face westward and moved to the faint tracks of the wagons. He decided to close his mind to everything. No!

Moss had said "Keep an eye open and stay low so's not to be seen . . . if'n ya wants to keep your topnotch."

He had to stay alert. Regardless of how he was feeling, he had to stay alert and stay awake. He could see nothing in any direction, but he figured it didn't mean much. Feeling a bit silly, he bent low and shakily ran back to the lower level of the stream. He wondered how far he'd be able to walk in his weakened condition.

When full sunlight came, he was able to move on rocks and sand but sometimes slipped into the shallow water. He kept to the water level as much as he could; sometimes he had brush and willows to shield him from view.

He kept moving but was forced to sit every hour or so till the sun was straight up. He knew he was a lot weaker than he should be, tired, and somehow sick. The fall, and the underground, had done something to him. He saw a patch of sand, sat, and ate jerky but saved the biscuits. He tasted the clear cold water from the stream.

He knew he had to get a skin to be able to leave the small creek. It was a worry. Shootin' the musket could be heard a long way and might well bring hostiles. He had decided to put off shootin' as long as possible.

He fell asleep in spite of his resolve to stay awake. In midafternoon, he continued up the stream. The waterway was twisting and turning among the sagebrush. He tried to keep low, and kept his mind on staying out of sight as much as he could. He thought of little else besides putting one foot ahead of the other.

The sun was sinking low. He'd spotted a patch of some sand out of sight and near the water. He made camp. He was exhausted and sat till he felt the cool of dusk and considered a fire. He knew it was out of the question. *Wait till I need one,* he thought. *Might be seen by hostiles.* No, he'd go slowly. It'd be lots cooler in a few weeks . . . if he survived that long! Moss had . . . and for many years. It was possible. Then he slept.

As the sun was coming up, he finished his jerky, a biscuit, and a long drink. He wished he had something to add to his meager diet. He started walking but stopped in midstride. The sun was no longer at his back. And it hadn't been since yesterday, he thought. Somewhere in the wandering streambed, he had come full north. He'd been walkin' away from the wagon trail for hours.

Standing on a sandstone shelf by the stream, he came to a firm decision. He had to have water, but he had no skin to carry it. He knew he was avoiding the idea of shootin' an animal to get a water skin. And he needed meat. He just wasn't ready to chance firin' the gun.

The facts were right there. He was afraid to take a chance. He mentally said good-bye to the wagons and continued walking north up the stream. It was a final farewell to his family. Then, he resolved, it'd not be *final.* Nor would seeing Sarah be final!

Something has to be north, he thought. So north it was.

Chapter 7

Food

The days had passed till Dan lost count. He idly wondered how many days it had been since he'd crawled from his underground prison. Was it as long as three weeks? All the jerky was gone. The naps had become fewer as the days passed, but he had to have food.

He'd barely managed to eke out the last few days. He'd killed a jack with a well-thrown rock, but now it was gone. He'd made a small fire to cook the rabbit. It was done in the daytime with small, dry pieces of wood—and it was built under some willows so the smoke got thinned out as Moss had said. And starting the fire with his flint and moss had taken less time than he'd remembered.

There'd been a few small fish, but they were too quick to get a hold on. He'd been able to trap only one—a small one—in a puddle, and cooked it over a tiny fire. He knew he'd starve if he had to get by on fish.

He was weak and exhausted. It was a great temptation to just give it all up and go to sleep—maybe forever. Colleen made him get back up. He'd return her scarf. He'd find his family.

Earlier, he had seen two deer drinking at the stream, but he was afraid of shooting. The noise might alert hostiles, but it

30

was time to take chances . . . if he was to live. And he needed a water skin if he was going to get away from the stream! Its water was about gone anyway. The musket had to be used. That was clear. He resolved to shoot the next animal he saw. He knew his life was at stake. If he waited too long . . .

The stream had become a small trickle, and he'd been climbing as he moved north. The time had become critical. He selected a shady spot under high brush and sat down to wait. He felt drowsy but no longer slept as soon as he closed his eyes.

Maybe the empty belly is helpin'.

He recalled his one important talk with Colleen along the trail.

"What are your plans?" she'd asked.

"n . . . no . . . not . . . su . . . sure . . . wh . . . wh . . . what . . . yo . . . you . . . me . . . me . . . mean."

"Do you plan to farm? What do you want to do in life?"

"Gu . . . gu . . . guess . . . I . . . nev . . . nev . . . never . . . tho . . . tho . . . thought . . . o . . . on . . . it."

Her question stuck in his head. In some ways, the deepest talkin' was done in silence. Some talkin' makes you think.

Belly pains brought him back to the present. He stretched out and drank the cold water. He was still bent over when he heard something. As slowly as he could, he lifted his head, fearing Indians. Not forty yards away, a young two-point buck was drinking in the stream.

Little by little, he edged the few inches to the musket and broke one of his powder pills into the pan. He'd gone over it a hundred times. If there was no dried mud or dirt in the barrel, he might have fresh meat! It was now—or starve. He slowly sighted on the buck; it was looking straight at him. He squeezed the trigger slowly. The flint flashed down and hit the frizzle, sending a spark to the pan, which flashed with a cloud of smoke before the powder below the ball ignited and forced the lead ball out with a roar. It seemed like it took forever. In reality, it had happened rapidly but forced Dan to hold on the target for a sight longer than was necessary with Josh's Hawkins.

When the smoke cleared, the small deer was on the ground. Dan had shot several deer back in Missouri but never where he might attract hostiles—and never when it was needed as desperately as this. Nervously, he stood and searched the hillside and his back trail. Had he been heard? Best to get that deer and get out of sight!

He dragged the small buck into the brush and dressed it out in short order. At the butchering, a passel of crows flapped back and forth, keeping sharp eyes on Dan's trophy. He wondered how far away wolves might be—or Indians.

He kept the bladder for his water skin, and carried a back quarter over his shoulder while moving up a small draw on the hillside away from the stream. He came across a rocky ledge somewhat concealed by brush and started his work. He left the smoothbore and turned back to bring another quarter up the hill with the leather bags. He was jumpy about leaving the gun but saw no other choice.

He knew he was in a dangerous and difficult place should Indians come upon him. He stopped every minute to study the hillside and ridge across the way. Finally, it was done, and he'd have to carry as much of the meat as he could. He'd have to leave the heavy hide. Steaks filled the treasure bag. The possibles bag carried balls, powder, flint, fire box, and the scarf. A rear quarter was carried over his shoulder.

He got to the bottom of a ravine and built his cooking fire while it was still daylight. There was a tiny trickle of cold water running down the ravine so he could clean up. Washing the bladder as best he could, he filled it with cold water. It was slow work, but it felt good to have a full water skin.

There were no trees or other foliage to thin the smoke. He had to take a chance; he used dry fuel and kept the fire small. It was the best he could think to do.

Finally, he had the steaks from the treasure bag cooked and had one in his belly. He'd carry the remaining hindquarter and cook meat off it to lessen the weight as he went.

Had he done all this without getting the notice of Indians? He carefully angled up the ridge. There was a slight gap at the top. He wouldn't be the only one seekin' to stay from getting sky lined on the ridge tops. He could see no tracks in the small gap and was able to slip over, feeling confident he hadn't been seen.

He surveyed the vast country ahead. Miles of timber! And, behind the timber, tall, snow-covered mountains. They stood there cold and threatening.

There had to be white folks somewhere to the north . . . he hoped.

Chapter 8

The Cave

He knew he was in for rain—maybe lots of rain by the looks of the black sky stretchin' out to the mountains. He could see a dark spot on a cliff face not too far away, so he determined to give it a closer look.

It had been slow going with the flintlock, bags, and meat. He was worn down and needed a dry place to rest. He was still weak from the sickness. But he thought that he might be getting better with the fresh meat.

Coming closer, he saw it was a cave. He grew cautious as he neared. It was recessed deeply in the cliff's face and was mighty dark. He placed his burdens on the ground and pitched several rocks into the cave. If there was a bear or varmint, they'd not been disturbed by the rocks. At least, nothing came out.

He carried his meat into the recess but didn't venture beyond a few feet of the overhang. He'd be out of the rain, but there was no way he was lookin' for more darkness! He wished he could hang the hindquarter somewhere but set it on a rock ledge. He sat nearby and kept the musket and bags close.

Glad for a rest, he ate another steak and drank from his water skin. He felt that he was making great progress. He'd managed food and had water he could tote with him. He'd be out of the rain. Still he worried about a bear or varmint in the rear of the cave. He took up the old musket and rubbed animal grease over all the metal parts. Rust was already appearing, but the grease would help.

He knew he'd accomplished several lifesaving things. Best of all, he hadn't been detected by hostiles. It would be an uphill trail when the snows began to fall. How would he manage without warm furs? Where could he find shelter? How would he be able to keep a fire burning during the freezin' times?

He leaned back against the rock wall and felt a familiar lump in his coat. He pulled the rock from his coat pocket. He fingered it idly. Strange rock. It was much too heavy for such a small rock, much like his thoughts.

Chapter 9

Sam

He turned over, rested his head on an arm, and slept as the rain came. Sometime during the night, he was dimly aware of a slight noise. Half awake, he listened but heard nothing and, figurin' it was a rodent, slept.

He woke feeling much refreshed in the dim light of early morning. He stretched and reached for the water skin. When he saw the open treasure bag, he panicked. He carefully reached for the flintlock. Very slowly, he fingered a powder pill in his coat pocket and slipped it down to the musket. He tore the small paper packet and dumped it onto the pan of the old gun. It would be ready to fire by merely pulling back on the hammer.

He stood as if to stretch, and casually turned to face the darkness. He was sure someone was in the cave with him! He faced the darkness and searched, never taking his eyes away from the darkness.

He felt like he stood there for nearly an hour. *Was that a movement?* He tensed and kept the musket barrel pointed to the spot where he thought he'd seen motion. Then he saw the outline of a small figure in the blackness. Slowly his eyes made out what seemed to be a midget. Or was there some tribe of small Indians out in the wild?

He was stunned when the small figure edged forward with arm extended as if offering some gift. Dan saw a tiny sliver of something in the hand of a child wearing a skin robe. He was certainly an Indian! Dan slowly lowered the gun as the child advanced, still holding his arm out. Dan reached out and the Indian put the thing into his hand. It was all that was left of a steak.

Was the child alone? How had he come to be in this cave? It made no sense. After a time, Dan sat back in his place. The child walked forward and sat beside him. No word had been uttered, but the child was looking at the water skin. Dan handed it to the boy.

The child swiftly untied the gut and started drinking. Finally, the boy lowered the skin and deftly retied the gut. Dan smiled. After weeks alone, he was sittin' beside another human bein'. Child or no, he was no longer alone! Ah! Would his people be lookin' for him? What then?

Dan was confused. What should he do? *Leave the boy? Did he have plans?* He stood and began picking up gear. The boy picked up the skin and hung it from his small neck.

"Gonna help? This mean you're travelin' with this, son?" Dan spoke for the first time in what seemed forever. He liked the sound. He considered that he'd come to terms with somethin' along the trail, but he wasn't sure what it might be.

The boy was a puzzle. He was small, but he seemed older than his size.

"Got to call you something. How's about *Sam*? Don't mind Sam? So be it, Sam. Let's move out."

He stepped out of the cave and viewed the remaining clouds. He studied the snow-covered mountains and knew he was movin' into fall's cold weather.

Chapter 10

Timber

He started down the slope toward the timber. Sam was right on his heels. *How long had Sam been in that cave?* It was strange. Maybe someday he'd unravel the mystery. He was satisfied the boy caused him no delay. He moved right on Dan's heels.

Before long, they entered the timber. Sam quickly moved forward and beckoned to Dan to follow. Soon they were on a trail that afforded swift travel. They had traded places, and the boy led the way.

Dan was somewhat amazed and more than a little worried. Was he bein' led to the boy's tribe? Then what? *Would they make quick end to this white man?*

Dan called a halt, and they ate deer steak and drank water. Dan pointed to the boy and said, "Sam." He reversed his finger and said, "Dan." He repeated this several times. The boy seemed to understand and tried to intone the word "Sam" with varied success. He did a bit better with "Dan" which came out "Dawnah." Dan knew he'd have trouble with the Indian's lingo.

Soon the pair was back on the trail, and the boy seemed to move faster. Dan hurried to keep up; the deer meat weighed heavily on his shoulder. He struggled with the heavy flintlock.

After a couple of hours, Sam moved off the trail, climbing through the timber. Dan followed with misgivings.

Suddenly, Dan caught a smell of something bad. Sam had stopped by a cold campfire. Beside it, a still figure was wrapped in a buffalo robe. An ancient Indian had been dead for at least three or four days. The boy gazed on the old man for a brief moment before turning and retracing the way they'd come. Dan's belly was upset, and he recoiled from the smell. He cleared his mind of thoughts of dead people and followed the Indian back to the faint trail.

Moving mostly north, they made good time. They came onto a spring. Dan filled the water skin after drinking deeply of the sweet water. They sat for a time and rested. Dan figured they had two hours to find a camping place. He wished he had a warm coat. It was gettin' downright chilly. The boy didn't seem bothered.

Chapter 11

Improvements

In the week since they'd left the cave, except for a brief shower, they'd had good weather. It was beginning to get colder.

Dan buttoned his buckskin jacket during the day and shivered at night. It was time for fires. He might have used the deerskin to fashion a coat but knew it would have been too dangerous. He'd been out in the open in low sagebrush. He would have had to scrape the hide and stake it out and, somehow, softened it. No. That hadn't been an option. And, besides, the deer hide would not make a really warm winter coat.

He was glad for the absence of the deer leg over his shoulder. They'd eaten it after slicing steaks off around the late noonday fires. He wished he could keep a fire during the night, but he was not yet willin' to take the chance. Moss had warned that fire at night was a beacon—often for trouble. He was puzzled. He'd heard that Indians didn't much like night fightin', but maybe they'd know where you were come daylight.

He smelled decay coming from the treasure bag where the last deer steak was packed. He knew it was time for fresh meat.

His chance came sooner than expected, and he was totally unprepared. It was drizzlin', and the pan of the old flintlock was wet—even if he'd had a powder pill in his hand, which was not the case. He ruefully watched the large deer bound away into broken timber. He wished he had something to cover the pan to keep it dry. He resolved to find a solution.

Before long he'd fashioned a leather thong which he tied over the pan tight enough to keep powder in and rain out. Would it work?

They'd come upon thick blackberry bushes though all the berries were long gone, Then, as they circled the brambles, Sam threw himself on the ground before Dan. There, he saw the bear cubs and the enormous grizzly rising to her full height with a loud growl. He quickly swung the the old flintlock on the bear—while pushing the leather thong off with a silent prayer that powder had remained in the pan—and pulled the trigger. He dropped to the ground alongside Sam as the smoke cloud dispersed in the small wind. As the smoke drifted away they lay in amazement. The bears were gone. Dan would never understand what had happened. Had he wounded the monstrous bear or, had the roar of the gun with its mushroom of smoke spooked the animal away? Sam was watching Dan as he reloaded the gun. He was clearly in wonder at the white man's power.

Conversely, Dan was in wonder at Sam's magic in holding consistently to the northwest. The small Indian was following an invisible trail. To where, Dan was uncertain.

Sam never hesitated when they came to a branch in the nearly invisible trail. Dan decided to stick with Sam. At least he knew where he was going. Dan would just have to take his chances. Besides, he he knew he'd be unable to survive a winter by himself.

It was too cold. Sam helped by getting dry ground wood and setting up stones that collected the heat of the fire. He showed Dan how to build a fire near to the rock face of a cliff to reflect the heat back.

Dan had come to see that he was the child in the wild; this Indian was right at home and knew how to live here. Every day, he'd show Dan how little Dan knew, and the two formed a bond of understanding and trust. They'd been able to communicate with hand signs and gestures.

At the evening campfire, Sam practiced saying "Dan." It came out "Danay," which suited Dan. Sam made an effort to say his name for Dan's benefit; it sounded to Dan like the boy was saying "Ca hoo ca," but he wasn't sure. Nonetheless, he tried to repeat the tones and watched Sam grin.

They were hungry. The meat was gone. They drank water and went on. Dan knew it was long overdue to shoot an animal. They were near starved. They progressed through a thinly timbered area which had burned many years before. A few old dead-falls still showed the signs of the burn. And brush was thick but allowing passage. Where growth had not been touched by the fire there was dense brush and large timber which shielded the sun and blinded them from the sky. In these areas, they often had either to go around the dense growth or spend hours climbing and beating a way through. It was easy for Dan to lose direction when they were covered by dense timber. Which was north or west—or even south or east—was often a mystery at such times. Sam, however, invariably held to the northwest as if by instinct.

Travel had become exhausting for Dan, and he found himself falling behind. Sam would periodically wait and patiently sit while Dan collected himself and regained strength. Going up was sometimes impossible on the severe steepness of the foothills around the nearby mountains. The thick timber and brush were impenetrable.

Dan awoke and knew he was freezing. He had to have fire. He shook badly as he fumbled with the icy tin and the piece of flint. He knew he'd have to go careful and slow. How long could he last in this cold? He saw that Sam was walking back and forth shaking and desperately trying to stay warm. The cold had snuck in during the night and would soon have killed them. Sam had gathered a handful of dry twigs and old parts of pinecone and deadwood. Thankfully, the flame caught at first try and they soon had a roaring fire. The unlikely companions huddled together around the fire until first light.

They were soon on the trail moving fast to keep warm. Dan was frightened. How long could they travel in this condition? They had to have shelter. Sam led them rapidly on the dim trail heading north but a bit west. How could the small Indian manage in this freezing cold? But he seemed to do better than Dan. It was a puzzle.

Sam clearly had a destination in mind and held to the northwest. Dan meanwhile fought his weakness and wondered if he were getting sick again. The cold surely didn't help, he thought.

The trail they followed was one not followed easily by whites, Dan knew. It was extremely faint and wandered through rough brush, timber, and mountainous ridges and valleys. Dan saw the reason for the torturous routing; it led from water to water and camp area to camp area. The camp areas were almost all in areas of concealment where fires were not easily seen. Trailing over the higher areas avoided moving where they could be sky lined. Dan was learnin', but he wondered if it was enough. He reflected that he'd almost sure to have become lost without sense of direction but for Sam. He'd have circled back on himself and died of thirst, or starvation, and exhaustion. He was honest enough to face this fact squarely. Without the small Indian, *he'd die*. Perhaps he still would. He still fought weakness and the freezing cold.

Another deer soon fell to the old musket, and he was startled to see how fast Sam ran to the downed animal. Clearly he had been around firearms. They'd pushed starvation away just in time.

Chapter 12

Visitors

The weather had magically changed bringing a warm spell. Well, thought Dan, it's still cold but not a killing cold.

They were comfortable and well fed as they leaned back against the large rock before the fire. Sam was practicing his English and saying "Dan" and "Sam" in his guttural tones.

Dan was relaxing and enjoying the welcome heat. They'd eaten roasted steaks and felt content. He closed his eyes and heard Sam saying their names. All of a sudden, Sam's voice stopped in the middle of a name. Dan's eyes snapped open; Sam was staring up with wide eyes.

"Well, well. What we got here?"

Dan's eyes focused on a large dim figure just beyond the fire. He reached for the old musket but was stayed when the voice came louder.

"Wouldn't do that, boy!" Dan froze. The voice came even louder. "Seth, bring those hosses in. We got an invite to eat!"

A younger man appeared, leading two saddled horses. He ground hitched them a few yards from the fire, loosened the cinches, and came up to the fire.

"Say, why you travelin' with an injun brat? You a squaw man?"

Dan didn't answer.

The other man advanced to the fire and sat with his rifle pointed at Dan.

Dan was angry that he'd been walked up on like this and caught dead to rights. And he liked neither man. They were dirty, surly, and arrogant. The pointed gun left no doubt who was in charge. Their intent sure wasn't something good.

The younger man had a slack stupid look mixed with a sneer on his face. The other man had the meanest face Dan had ever seen. His eyes were dark, hard, and deadly—like rattlesnake eyes.

Sam remained seated by Dan.

"I'm Seth," said the man. He had a pistol stuck in the belt of his filthy buffalo coat. "Yes, siree. We're right pleased to meet ya. Now, let's have some meat, boy."

Dan moved to the deer hanging from a tree, hacked off a couple of steaks, and stuck them on a spit over the fire.

As the meat sizzled, the two men crowded close to the fire. Their filthy hair hung down to their shoulders, and they had thick black beards. There was nothing clean or appealing about either man.

"Where you men be traveling?" Dan asked.

Seth grinned. "Well, boy, we be traveling where you been. Good to finally meet up with ye."

How long had they been followin'? What they wanted wasn't a good thing to think about.

Seth said, "Jethro, I just got to peek in these bags and see what gold these two be carryin'." He picked up the treasure bag, which was filled with cooked steaks. He tossed it down and reached for the possibles bag as Dan quickly grabbed for it. He was immediately facing the pistol from Seth's belt. He pushed back, leaving the bag where it was.

"That's better," said Seth. "Jest sit, boy." He dumped the bag on the ground and stirred it with the toe of his boot. He reached down and picked up the scarf. Before Dan considered what he was doin', he snatched the scarf from Seth's hand.

This time, the gun was in his face—with the hammer clicked back.

"Seth! Don't," Jethro said.

Seth was shaking. Dan knew he'd barely missed havin' his brains blown out.

"This injun's people might be close by. We'll go careful a while," Jethro grunted.

Seth said, "What's the brat doin' with ya?"

Jethro pulled a steak from the spit, and held out the stick for Seth to take it. The younger man began chewing on hot meat.

Dan was angry. He'd slipped up all around. Moss would have been disgusted. How could he have been so careless? He and Sam had been followed.

The only sound was the crackle of the fire. At least, he had the scarf.

Chapter 13

Well Away

The old flintlock rested on the ground near to the older man. Both men snored.

Dan was filled with rage but knew he had to think and go slow. He had to get away from these vultures—and quick!

Drawing up one plan after another, he finally reached out to touch Sam who was behind him. But he wasn't there! His eyes searched everything he could see in the firelight. Nothin'. Then he felt a hand touch him on the shoulder. Dan swung back, and the boy pointed behind him where the two horses stood!

Dan was never able to convince himself that the boy had been able to retrieve the horses unheard, but he never again doubted the ability of Indians to steal horses. They were masters! That night would always be a joyous memory for Dan. He quietly collected his gear while Sam fetched the flintlock without a whisper of sound.

Dan tightened the cinches, and they were well away with not a sound from the sleeping men except their snoring.

He felt a grim satisfaction as they rode. They'd been held up by arrogant thieves behind guns. Now he was regretting leaving that Hawkins Jethro was carrying. But they'd done well, Dan knew, and because of Sam.

Riding till the sun was straight up, they ground hitched the horses, ate meat, and drank water. As they sat, Dan reached over to Sam with an outstretched arm. He solemnly shook Sam's hand as the lad grinned. They'd come out on top because of Sam, and Dan knew it.

They had horseflesh! The miles flew behind them. Dan had learned a lesson and kept a keen eye on their back trail. He suspected that the two men might well hesitate to follow because of Sam. They were sure not wantin' to meet up with Sam's tribe and had no idea where that might be.

But I don't know where that might be, either! Dan shook his head and followed Sam's lead. The boy went swiftly, knowing exactly where he was going.

Two days later, they'd climbed close to the mountains. The snow came and they moved through large snowflakes. Dan had only his light buckskin jacket and shivered constantly. Sam was surely cold, he thought, but the lad rode on seeming unconcerned.

Sam smelled smoke! He soon saw tepees; Sam began a mad gallop into the village. He was yipping at the top of his lungs as he galloped through the village and back to Dan. Indians appeared among the tepees with mouths open in astonishment. It was a total bedlam as Indian children began jumping up and down and screeching loudly among yapping dogs. The galloping boy and the white man had the village in a state of amazement.

Sam led Dan to a tepee with a muscled Indian and a beaming squaw. Sam had turned solemn while speaking to the large man. He turned and nodded at Dan and gestured for him to step near. The large Indian pulled Dan close in a bear hug. The Indian woman ran to Sam and was hugging him and laughing in her joy. So Dan knew that Sam was home and all was well.

The days ahead were a wonder to Dan. He was able to converse with the Indians because Sam had taught Dan enough sign language for rudimentary communications. Sam translated a great deal simply because he had come to know the white man so well.

Dan learned rituals like smoking the long-stemmed pipe in the chief's tepee. He came to know that the Indians had a great sense of humor. They were highly efficient at living in the cold country. The squaws managed the village and the children so well that he never heard a baby cry during the nighttime. The Indian boys played important games with bow and arrows. The older boys learned wonderful horsemanship.

Dan learned to hunt buffalo with the hunting parties. Sam's mother presented him with a beautiful buckskin outfit to replace his tattered clothes. Sam's aunt and uncle presented him with a wonderful bearskin coat. Another squaw made a pair of elk skin boots for him. The latter gift made him nervous as she smiled at him often, and Sam said her brave had died in battle. She was alone now.

Dan was adopted into the tribe; he formed friendships and began learning skills he'd only dreamed about. He was given training in the tracking of animals. He was amazed by how little he knew of living in the wilderness—it was simply home to the Indians and not a source of fear. They proceeded with caution because there were other tribes with whom they were at war.

The snow continued to come down, and Dan learned the joy of living in his own tepee with Sam. It was warm and clean. They practiced language for hours. Dan learned to speak some of Sam's language but resorted to hand signs a great deal, too.

Dan learned the mystery of Sam's presence in the cave. He'd gone back to be with his grandfather who remained behind to die. He wasn't missed for several hours. The tribe had to go on. It seemed cruel to Dan, but it was the custom of the tribe. The welfare of the tribe came first. Dan nodded. He could understand. The wagons had to go on without him for the same reason. Maybe that was when he'd started really growin' up.

Sam's grandfather was near death when Sam heard horses coming through the brush. He'd tried to hide but was seen and the chase was on. Seth and Jethro hadn't seemed to recognize Sam as the same boy they'd followed through the brush. Sam had run fast enough to avoid the white men and, finally, reached the cave.

Sam explained the custom of old people, as death approached—and it was on the trail—choosing to remain behind to die alone.

Dan was given great esteem in the tribe. He'd returned with the chief's son. And Sam had given great credit to Dan for their welfare on the long trail home.

In the winter, Sam and Dan were rarely apart. They'd become like brothers and shared everything. Dan had taught the younger lad to shoot the flintlock, though he only shot twice due to the lack of lead balls. Dan knew he had to preserve as many as possible. He'd used one to shoot a young buffalo close up behind the front quarter—a good heart shot for a light shooting gun.

He slept a good deal when it snowed, keeping a warm fire in the tepee. One day after a long session with Sam and the bow and arrow, he retired to the tepee and quickly nodded off. He dreamed of Josh and Mary. Colleen and he were walking together behind the wagon. She'd laughed at something he'd said, and he wanted terribly to take her hand but couldn't work up the nerve. Then Sam was shaking him. Dan thought it must be time for the wagons to move on.

When he was awake, they went out for a tribal feast.

Chapter 14

Good-byes

The winter had not been severe and, before Dan knew it, it was spring. He felt content with the winter. He'd hunted with the Indians, learned much of their language, and seen what great horsemen the Indians were. They rode close on a buffalo and shot with a strong bow in behind a front quarter to bring the buffalo down. Dan saw it was as good as his musket. A dead buff was a dead buff. And he had warm buckskins and knee boots. He'd survived.

Sam was the son of the tribe's chief, or, at least, one of the chiefs in the tribe. Dan wasn't sure which chief Sam's father was but had the idea he was a main chief of the tribe. There was a war chief, and the medicine man was a sort of chief. It got confusin'. He thought there was a chief of the hunt.

He knew a few of the braves looked at him with suspicion, and a few clearly disliked him. But many seemed to like him and welcomed Dan into their tepees for meals and visits.

When the day came for the tribe to move on, Dan met with Sam to say his good-byes. He knew that Sam would always remain his friend should they meet again. Dan had never had a brother but felt he had one now. He still had no clear idea of Sam's age.

The Indians didn't say "good-byes" in the fashion of whites. They just parted. He found this especially hard to understand.

Dan headed north toward a small camp of whites. Sam's father had said it was about one moon's fast travel by horse. Sam looked at his provisions and felt equipped for anything. He wished he had some more lead balls, but maybe he could get more at the encampment of whites. He wondered why they were there.

The parting with Sam sore wrung his heart. Here was a man—not a child—who'd guided him safely through the wilderness day after long day. He'd gone hungry and thirsty with Dan. He'd rescued them from the hands of thieves and, likely, killers. He'd brought them to safety and shared his home with Dan through the long winter. Now he had to go on alone. He'd miss Sam. He'd miss him badly.

As Dan moved alone through the timber, his thoughts turned to his family in Oregon Country. He knew they'd have gone through Fort Boise somewhere west and, likely, south, though he was uncertain exactly where *he* was. If all had gone well, they'd be settled somewhere in Oregon. He dreamed of them often, especially Colleen, and wondered if she missed him as much as he missed her.

The Indians had told him of strange things in the north country where water shot up toward the sky. And they told of springs that remained wonderfully warm through the cold of winter. It was all unlikely to be, he thought, but Indian ways proved pretty sound when you saw them through. So maybe these things really were as they said.

He had a sense of where he was, but it was only a rough map in his mind. Besides, the few weeks of travel to the white's camp was too much to resist. So he set the beautiful peaks to the front and headed north.

Chapter 15

Gold

Dan moved through some rough country, but the chief's directions were good. Again, Dan smelled smoke before seeing anything. When he did see, he wasn't greatly impressed. There was one low, long log cabin. The roof was covered with sod, and wildflowers were growing there. A thin stream of smoke was drifting from a clay chimney on the backside. A rough pole corral was attached to the end of the cabin. And that was it. The strange thing was that it appeared to be old.

After hailin' the cabin with no response, he dismounted and pounded hard on the one door. No one home, he thought, and unsaddled, putting his horse in the corral with three other horses. Then he sat on a log in front of the cabin.

He'd resolved to go carefully in this, his second contact with whites since the wagons. It was midday, and he munched on his jerky. He kept the musket across his lap with powder in the pan. He closed his eyes and slumbered. Suddenly, he heard a horse's hoof click against a stone on the hillside behind the cabin. He was instantly awake.

Dan eased the musket so it appeared to be a casual thing on his lap, but it was tilted a bit when the horse rounded the cabin. The small horse was mounted with the most comical sight Dan had ever seen. On the horse was a long, lean man whose legs nearly touched the ground. He appeared to move his feet with the horse's hooves as if they walked in unison.

The face was long and lean, too, and matched the man's figure. His smile triggered a smile on Dan's face. The man glanced at the musket that was not pointed *directly* at him but wasn't far from it.

Speaking around an unlit pipe, the man said, "Well, ya all go sort of careful, don't ya!" He was still smiling through his bushy beard; his unclean, yellowed teeth gripped the pipe stem. Dan set the musket upright against the log and rose. Dan felt comfortable with this man.

Dismounting was likewise comical; the tall man looked to be merely steppin' over his horse. He extended a long arm to Dan and said, "Welcome to 'Nowhere.' I'm Jonathan Bills."

Dan was tickled to hear English talk again and laughed at the name of the camp. He shook hands and said, "I'm Dan Fitzgerald."

"What brings ya to Nowhere, Dan?"

Dan gave a brief answer, which just noted his winterin' with the Indians.

"Wintered with the Shoshones, did ya? Well, they's good people, general. Going to get a claim?"

"What's a claim?"

Jonathan threw a thumb back to the hillside above and back of the cabin. "There's color showin' purty fair if 'n ya dig hard. Chance to make a fair poke."

He soon met Jeff and Humphrey. Jeff, a small, quiet, red-haired man, rarely said a word not necessary to his diggings. Humphrey was big, heavy, black haired, and talked his head off. In fact, he was given to talking to himself all day long. Sounded like there were two men in his hole for all the arguing he did with himself. And he was obsessed with a tall pine tree on his claim.

Humphrey said, "That tree needs fallin' so's to cross the creek and divert water nearer to the holes."

Thus started Dan's becoming a miner of sorts. He was shown a piece of ground above the small creek and joined the community of three. He borrowed a shovel and wooden bucket, which he had to return often to the owner. But it permitted him to start a hole where he carried dirt to the stream and washed the dirt in a pan. It was tedious work. Hard, especially on the back. But Dan was a quick learner. He took the old pan and kept at it. Little by little, his small leather sack was filling with small nuggets and dust.

The others showed Dan how to make a wooden shovel. He felt good to be with these lonely men in the timbered wilderness in the corner of nowhere. *Well named*, Dan thought. It sure was a godforsaken place on a hillside among the pines.

The four men slept on the dirt floor of the cabin—each with feet extended to the fireplace even though no fire was burning. They mostly ate their meat and wild onion outside since the cabin had no window and was dark with just the door open to the light.

One day, Jonathan rode off in the early morning without a word. Come noontime, the three men saw him riding up the hillside. His hat was cradled against his chest and clearly carried something.

He did his silly step-down from the horse and said, "Come on, boys! Got some berries."

The berries were a fine treat, and they devoured the blackberries in short order. Jonathan had clearly had his fill; purple stains covered his lips and hands.

In return for the loan of tools, Dan fetched deer meat for the camp. They all worked from dawn to dark on the hillside. Jonathan told Dan how he'd wandered on the crude cabin one day while prospecting and knew it was a miner's abode from the few tools hanging on cabin logs.

"No one were livin' here for some time," said Jonathan. "And I found a hole up yonder on the hill and some color. So's I jest settled. Than here come two more destitutes who wanted for to dig. Then you shows up. Gettin' to be a downright crowded township here in Nowhere."

Dan was curious about why the three men all had pipes in their teeth from morning to night. They had no tobacco, but they still sucked on the pipes. They were good, easy company. He worked hard to show something for his labor, and his poke slowly filled through the summer.

Dan was accepted as a grown man. He was sure a man on his own and was taken at face value. Jeff and Humphrey wore buckskin like Dan's while Jonathan wore tattered cotton except for a buckskin jacket. The pants hung only down to his ankles and his sleeves were long gone with just tattered threads hanging below his shoulders.

In late summer, Humphrey found a rusted ax stuck in a tree. He gleefully honed the blade till he had it sharp and began hacking at the tall pine that offended him.

Chapter 16

Funeral in Nowhere

Humphrey told them he had it all planned out. He'd hacked at the tree for a couple of hours and figured it was due to fall. He'd gathered his fellow citizens to view the great falling-down event. When the tree started swaying and a loud crackling noise came, Humphrey stood by and watched with pride and joy. He was shocked to see the cut end bounce and swing square into his chest.

They buried him near the cabin. Jonathan had a small dog-eared testament and read over the grave as each man stood bareheaded. Jonathan ended his reading and said, "He died a happy dyin'. God bless! Amens."

Dan was thinkin' about his parent's burial and remembered the long readin' the preacher had done before they'd lowered the pine boxes into the deep graves. He'd wanted to protest but couldn't get a word out of his mouth. He'd wanted badly to yell *no*, but he couldn't—and he felt guilt that they'd died and not him. They were good, and it wasn't right that they'd died. Humphrey had died happy. Dan's Ma and Pa had died scared at leavin' their children alone.

They buried Humphrey in a shallow grave with rocks piled atop to keep varmints from digging him up. Jonathan placed a small piece of old cloth over Humphrey's smashed face; Dan wondered if that was custom or because he was so smashed. Soon they were back to work digging.

That evening, they took stock of what small belongings Humphrey had. Foremost, of course, was his poke. They talked as how would they divide the poke with no scales. The surprise was Jonathan's idea that they draw for high card as he produced a tattered old deck. So it was agreed.

Jonathan spread the cards out on a blanket on the dirt floor. Jeff pulled a card and snorted as he held up a dirty deuce of clubs. Dan picked up a card and turned up a badly smudged nine of diamonds. Jonathan reached into the pile of old cards and had an eight of diamonds, likewise dirty. He laughed and tossed the large poke to Dan. Dan pocketed the poke without sayin' near, far, or thankye.

"How's about that hoss a his?" Jeff said.

And they thought it a grand idea to draw high card again. This time, Jeff won himself an extra horse when he drew a king of hearts. Last was the one thing Dan for sure wanted—a Hawkins rifle with ball and powder. Jeff again drew first and turned a four of spades. He didn't seem much to care. He'd wanted that horse. Dan drew a ten of spades. Jonathan picked up a ten of hearts.

So the two drew again. Dan won the Hawkins when he picked up a six of clubs and Jonathan turned a five of clubs.

Jonathan grinned and said, "I never did do good at the pasteboards."

Dan smiled and said, "Sure be good to say so long to that old flintlock though it did a purty fair job for bein' so old and slow."

The next day, Dan carried the Hawkins up the hillside, and loaded it up. Jonathan and Jeff stopped by to see the shooting. Dan picked out a pinecone across the creek, figurin' it to be maybe fifty yards off. Jonathan thought maybe sixty.

Dan pulled down and blew it clean away. "Straight shootin' enough for me," he said.

While the men went back to digging, Dan washed the barrel at the creek and laid it out in the warm sun to dry. He'd take care of this gun for sure.

Chapter 17

A Killing

Dan's summer mining work came to an end a few weeks later. He was feeling wealthy with no place to buy. He had two pokes, a horse, and a good Hawkins rife in fifty caliber. He'd hung the old flintlock on a wall of the cabin and left it there. He'd made himself a scabbard for the Hawkins so the butt end came up and passed by his thigh. After a bit a practice, he could fetch it out tolerably fast.

The two men shook hands with Dan, and he headed west and south for Fort Boise. Jonathan was going north with Jeff in search of richer diggings.

Dan loaded the Hawkins and set a cap on the nipple to fire it by just thumbing the hammer back and pulling the trigger. He was bound to not be taken by surprise again. No getting caught dead to rights again.

He was glad for the bearskin coat and avoided fires for as long as possible. He'd been lucky so far, but he knew hostiles could make him a quick believer. He'd learned the hard way to keep a close eye on his back trail and paused often to search the country behind.

In spite of taking care, he was surprised as he rode out of some river willows into fast moving water.

"Well, look who come to bring back my stole' hoss!"

Dan carefully turned to see the sneering face of a man he knew all too well.

Seth pulled the pistol from his belt and snapped a shot at Dan from his jumping horse.

Dan snatched the Hawkins from the scabbard, thumbing back the hammer as another ball whizzed by his head. Dan's horse was squirming around like Seth's in the swift water, but he knew right then that Seth would ride no further.

Dan took careful aim and shot Seth out of the saddle. He quickly set a new ball on the powder he'd put down the barrel.

Jethro yelled, "Seth! Where you be? Are you all rights?"

Dan had the ramrod in the barrel when Jethro galloped out of the willows.

"You're a dead man! You kilt my brother, you varmint, and now's you're dead!" Jethro pulled his rifle up.

"No! Tain't so, son! I got a bead on you. Pull the rifle down quick."

Jethro was enraged, but knew someone had the drop on him. He was looking to find the owner of the voice but had no luck.

Dan had his Hawkins ready and held it on Jethro as he rode back into the willows from whence the voice had come. Sure enough, Moss sat on his horse with a rifle on Jethro.

Dan could hardly believe his eyes. Moss! And just when he needed a friend!

"Well, I thought you be in the Willamette! Where's your Ma and Pa?"

They rode back through the willows and crossed over the river on sandbars in shallow water. After a few miles of climbing out of the river valley, they lit for a spell.

Moss saw that Dan was looking pretty peaked—as if he was going to heave up his guts.

"Well, son, you did good."

"Never want to ever kill any other human being."

Moss looked close at Dan and said, "You kill to protect a life, and sometimes it's your own, but you do right to do it."

Dan felt depressed but put off his brooding. He filled Moss in on his separation from the wagons and his doings.

"You're alive, son! But ye been a mite lucky! You did right back at the river. He'd a kilt you for shore. Ne'er wait til' a varmint's got a gun in his hand. Shoot first and straight."

When Dan related his gold venture, Moss asked, "Where in the hell is Nowhere?"

Dan said it was back eastward a skip or jump of maybe ten days.

Moss said he'd get there one day just to see the sights. He had noted the lack of stutter in Dan but decided it was not his business and never mentioned it. He was surprised how the lad had grown. He was now taller than Moss—and tough! Moss knew a tough man when he saw one!

Moss continued talking like he'd never had a chance. "Mind a mountain man a twenty or so years back by name a Jed Smith who were more places in the West than even the buffalo knowed. But he went away and didn't come back, so's I reckon the injuns got 'em. An' you needs to meet old Jim Bridger and Beckworth. An old Tom Fitzpatrick. Oh! You needs to meet up with tha meat a these here mountains!"

Chapter 18

Fort Boise

Dan had no doubts about seeing Jethro again. He'd keep a keen eye peeled. Moss was just the non-stop-talkingest man he had ever known. It was as if he'd come bound to talk and just had to catch up. It was stored up, sort of, and just gushed out hour after hour.

Dan thought it strange that Moss never mentioned his family or where he came from back in the States.

"Yes, siree! Ran smack inta a grizzly back in '25. He near tore my hide cle'r off a'for I got my toothpick into him real good. Thought I were done fer!"

Moss's stories seemed fair to being endless, thought Dan. On they rode, scanning the country for likely ambushes. The miles passed quickly.

Dan blamed himself for making Moss careless. They were crossing a river and holding tight to the horses' tails. Neither of the two had ever learned to swim, so they let the horses do it and just held on.

They were coming to the shore on the far side when a shot rang out. Moss was in front of Dan, and he saw Moss holding on as he made the shore. Dan figured that he'd gone untouched. It was only when he got out of the current that he saw the blood smeared on the grass and knew Moss had taken a ball.

Dan figured he couldn't have been hit badly since Moss had kept a hold of his horse till he made the bank and crawled into the grass. Dan just followed the blood smears on the grass.

Crawling, he came upon Moss down on the grass. His breathing was really shallow. Dan had to keep low in the grass, but he got Moss onto his back. It was a head wound, and the bleeding was heavy. Dan knew he had to do something quick and clamped a handful of grass over the wound. He felt a large bump within the wound.

Soon, he couldn't hear Moss breathing, and Dan was sure he'd died. He had a big problem. They needed a gun, but they were with the horses. Where were the horses? He did not want to leave Moss, but the killer was still out there somewhere.

He had to go careful. First, he had to get a gun. If he could lay sights on the damn horses! He moved back in the tall grass and took a chance, standing and peering over the grass. He got a quick look at the horses grazing nearby.

If he could get to a horse, he'd have a wet, unloaded rifle. He figured he'd bought a big parcel of trouble this time for sure. Then he heard a horse galloping off up the river. "Well, I'll be damned. The varmint got spooked."

He stood and saw Jethro's horse moving fast. For sure he'd killed Moss. Dan caught up the two horses and hurried back to Moss. He washed the wound. It looked bad. Real bad!

Hell, just a glancing hit on the noggin would kill you. This looks worse than a glancing hit.

Dan put his ear to Moss's chest but couldn't hear a heartbeat. And he wasn't breathing. Dan felt sick. "Killed because of me," Dan said. "He's got an unjust payment."

He buried Moss by the river with an old bandana over his face. He was buried shallow; Dan tried to find some rocks to put atop the grave but gave it up after a bit. He sat by the grave and tried to call up a prayer. *Wish Jonathan were here*, he thought. "Lord, he was a good man and friend. Amen."

He'd not given thought to fearing the dead body of Moss. Somehow it was different. He wished he had a box for Moss, but it was not to be out here in the wild.

He sat by the grave for a long spell, dreading leaving his friend. He gave thought to going after Jethro. He sure had killed a good man, and he needed to be stopped. He wondered if Moss was in a better place like the preacher had said at his parents' burials. If there was a better place than this, Moss would sure be talking and liking it because he sure enough loved these wilds.

Finally, he knew he had to move on. Death was final and couldn't be undone. He had to move on because he was alive. But the good-bye to Moss was hard.

Chapter 19

Tracking

Dan had learned a lot from Sam and his tribe. One of the best things was how to track. He knew he was small spuds alongside Sam. Those Indians were experts. Still, he'd learned a few things, he concluded.

Soon he cut the trail of the killer and, leading Max, rode as fast as he could. Tracking got slow in the rocky ground.

All right. I'll go slow and careful. But that varmint is mine.

In a week, he lost the trail. And, because of the time he'd used backtracking, he had to give it up. Hard, cold weather had come. He lit out for Fort Boise, hoping the killer was aiming for the same. But aiming was the best he could do in these rough mountains.

He became hopelessly lost. He stopped and resolved to find a clue as he'd done in the cave. There was no cool breeze to guide him. The breeze was a cold wind in the dense mountains and timber. He had to get out or perish. Darkness was approaching, so he found a low spot out of the wind and built a fire. He had found some rock and managed to get heat reflecting back, but it was still terribly cold. He shook as he sipped his coffee and reflected on his options. Jethro might have deliberately led Dan into this maze in hopes he'd die here. Jethro was capable of such a move, thought Dan.

The country was heavily timbered—up and down and sideways. In spite of every trick, he was often turned around and confused. He tried to head southwest, but on a cloudy day he often stayed put in a cold camp. He knew he was in a race with winter storms and had to press on as hard as possible. It was frustrating, and Dan carried a knot of fear inside.

One night he kept the fire burning especially large as a shield against the searing cold. In the dim first light he saddled Max, determined to find a way out. Holding to windswept areas he rode as near to east as he could manage. He just headed to the rising sun in the morning and put it to his back in the afternoon. It was uncertain but was a guide in the lack of others. Travel was slow, and he knew it was going to be tough for the horses to get through the deep drifts even taking turns. And, try as he would, he couldn't avoid deep snow.

In desperation, he dismounted and tried to break his way through a drift so the horses could follow. It was hopeless. He soon lay in exhaustion.

The following night found them around an inadequate fire. Dan slept only in snatches arising periodically to give melted water to the two horses. They needed feed, and there was none.

The dawning brought clear skies and a warming. They soon moved into a plateau where travel was good. Dan felt hope spring in his heart. He patted Max on his shoulder and went slow so as to spare the winded horses. Then he happened on grass which had not been totally covered by snow.

Dan dismounted and kicked snow off a patch of tall grass while the horses immediately began grazing. Dan resolved to remain in the area until the horses were rested and had plentiful time to graze on the grass. Meanwhile, he'd melt snow for the animals. They badly needed water.

Two weeks later they were out of the maze of mountains and able to head south. Then, Dan had a great stroke of luck. They'd gone an exhausting and cold three weeks before they stumbled on a river. Later, he found that he'd happened on the Boise River. He found intermittent wagon ruts in the snow. He followed these westward. Then, the ruts turned south and he found Fort Boise on the Snake River.

He was nervous about the Hudson's Bay Company, but the British traders were friendly. Jonathan and Moss had both assured him he'd like the British. He'd been doubtful.

He was treated to a feast hosted by the clerk of the fort, Francois Payette. They told him the last wagons had gone on to the Blues several weeks earlier. And they hadn't seen anyone fitting Jethro's description.

The magnet in Dan's head pointed west, but getting to the Willamette Valley meant he couldn't go directly west. One of the clerks had tried to explain the geography.

"You see, you head *north* so as to reach the Columbia and float *west* down the Big River to Fort Vancouver. Then, you go *south* into the Willamette Valley. It's sort of like going around a long building and coming down the other side. But, in this case, you're going around mountains."

They said the snow would be bad up in the Blues and travel would be tough to the Columbia. He decided to winter at the fort. If he got over the Blues, the British explained, he'd have to winter with the Whitman's before he'd get help from the wagon people rafting down the Columbia . . . provided some had wintered at The Dalles. In any event, rafting probably wouldn't be until early spring. So Fort Boise it was, he thought, though he'd like to press on.

His family never left his mind for long. He missed them. And he seemed so far away.

A tough winter came early, and his decision was made for him. He'd stay at Fort Boise. It was the second winter since he'd left Mary and Colleen at the wagon. It seemed longer to Dan. Had they made it to Oregon?

Chapter 20

Trapping

A grizzled old trapper named Jig came into the fort one day and, in boredom, Dan took to trapping with the old fellow. It was a tough life, he found, with small reward. His bearskin coat and fur-lined Indian boots were badly needed that winter.

He learned that shooting a fox or minx or wildcat with the .36 ball was how Jig got many of his prime furs. He had a packhorse loaded with plews, mostly beaver, which he'd traded at the fort.

One cold day, they were huddled under some trees with a big fire. They'd boiled coffee and ate fresh elk meat. Dan decided it was the best meat he'd set his lips to since the buffalo hump in Sam's village. Jig opined that the mountain cat was his choice for tasty meat.

Jig was heading for Oregon City on the Willamette in the spring. He'd never trapped below the Columbia but was bound to give it a try—provided the British didn't stop him. They claimed the valley below the big river was British fur territory. Well, he'd trade with them!

Dan half-listened as Jig mourned his bad luck up north and east of the Snake.

"Damn beav's most gone! An thiever's everywheres. Met one heading west a month or so's ago. Caught him one night and had to run him off quick. He were trying to steal my hides."

Dan woke up. Jig described the man, and Dan knew the old trapper had sure enough run into Jethro.

"Shore I got the drop on 'em as he were putting hand to my pack in the nighttime. Run 'em off pronto!"

Jethro was north and east of Dan. Maybe. He could be anywhere. Damn. Have to watch those river crossings really close. Jethro was partial to ambushing at river crossings. It made sense, though. Rifles would likely be wet and not loaded. *Makes a man real vulnerable*, Dan thought.

The winter slowly froze its way to an Indian spring. Things quickly started melting in a warm spell. The traders at the fort warned Dan that winter was coming back, and Dan stayed at the fort. A cold spell came and snow flew, but spring was coming.

Chapter 21

Crossing

Dan packed his gear on Max and rode out of Fort Boise. He swam the horses over the Snake, feeling safe as the fort was there, and he'd scouted it well.

He was across the river and a few miles west and upstream when he was hard hit. He had no idea what had happened. He awoke near a campfire. He felt hands raising his head, and might have sipped water, or maybe, it was all just a dream.

One day, he opened his eyes and saw poles. They were overhead and puzzled him mighty. What were they? He closed his eyes and slept.

In a few days, he knew the worst. He'd been ambushed. Jig found him not many hours later. Though he had not planned to, he'd tailed Dan by half a day out of Fort Boise. It was the luckiest break Dan ever had.

He was in a cabin where a friend of Jigs had taken to living. Jig was long gone on his way to Vancouver. His friend, Hayden, had taken Dan in and fed him deer broth. Dan was young and tough, and he was soon healing.

Hayden was a cheerful old mountain man and right glad to have Dan in his cabin. He just needed to have someone to gab with after a long winter alone. His cabin was ten miles or

74

so from the river, but he had no horse and was living along the wagon trail to the Columbia.

He told Dan how Jig had found him and brought him to the cabin. His horses were gone—along with the gear. All Dan had he was wearing along with his old knife.

It was summer before he was on his feet and moving good. It was a tough time. He had no doubt as to who had dry-gulched him. Sure enough, Jethro had taken to doing his killings at river crossings whenever possible, but would make do elsewhere if the occasion provided. Dan was angry. He'd scouted the crossing at the fort closely before he'd crossed over. And he'd kept his eyes open afterward. But he'd not seen sign of the bushwhacker. Jethro was plain good at his trade! Like a rattler in thick brush, Dan thought.

Dan had not even a small doubt as to what he'd do. Jethro had his pokes, his horses, his Hawkins, and Colleen's scarf. And he'd killed Moss. He knew he'd avenge Moss—and he'd have that scarf back!

Jig had told Hayden he'd found where the dry-gulcher had held down to make his shot. The tracks of the shooter had doubled back as if to cross back over the Snake heading east.

When Dan was ready to travel, he set out for Fort Boise on foot. He was unarmed except for the old knife. But it was less than ten miles to the fort. He left the fur coat for Hayden. It was all he had to give the old man to whom he owed his life. He would not forget Jig or Hayden.

Dan found a train of wagons on the west side of the Snake across from the fort. Indians were helping the settlers cross the river. He stopped to watch.

He looked with interest at the settlers. Their strange looks puzzled him. Had Ma and Pa and the folks he'd traveled with had this look? Then it came to him. They were carrying the marks of the States! They were wearing cotton clothes, and some of the men were clean shaven. They looked—not rich—but civilized!

He moved on as a few curious wagon folks peered at him closely. He wondered if he looked as downtrodden and penniless as he was. Well, that was no shame. And there was surely no shame in looking civilized; they'd not yet had a hard winter in this west country. They'd not had to live totally on the country—and *alone!*

Chapter 22

Mining Again

D an crossed to the Fort and was taken in. The clerks were amazed to see him alive. They'd talked to a traveler who had found the horses alongside a dead body. The man had described Dan. Then the traveler had quickly headed north up the east side of the Snake.

They told Dan that there were some tailings up north where color had been found. Dan lit out, hoping he could get another poke and—with luck—maybe Jethro!

By fall, he did have another poke. He'd taken up with some Chinamen and worked the tailings of white miners. Did right well, too. And he had an old buffalo coat that was heavy but warm. He made his way back to Fort Boise and swapped some gold for a good horse. A wagon man swapped a good Hawkins for some dust. The dust greatly excited the settlers, and a few headed off for the gold camps.

He put together a trail outfit and headed east. He hoped to find a trace of Jethro. He'd spent the summer north and found no trace of the critter. The West was a vast place, and it was filled up with mighty few folks. With white or Indian help, he'd sooner or later catch wind of the murdering thief. It was fall, and Jethro would soon be holing up somewhere.

He knew that trapping and prospecting were the most usual work for men and how they'd get together out in this wilderness. He looked for tailings and holes and Jethro. He wandered east up the Boise River toward Fort Hall. He knew that this was no time to be heading out on a long trail but was restless after a summer of getting well and washing dirt. Jethro would have to be wintering somewhere.

Since the mountains in the north were nearly impassable in winter, he headed up the Boise, following wagon ruts.

Jethro liked rivers for his work. He'd heed that.

He knew he'd have to follow the wagon ruts to find the Three Island Crossing he'd heard about at the fort. It was somewhere to the southeast where he'd hit the Snake. Funny, he thought, Ma and Pa and Colleen would have been going west on these ruts. When? Must be over three years ago. He found it was a fight not to turn back for Oregon Country but gritted his teeth and rode eastward.

From Three Island Crossing, he'd follow the Snake north and east to Fort Hall. Maybe Jethro had stopped there.

Moving slowly and carefully, he came up on the Boise River where the wagons had crossed over. He'd come up to the crossing on foot after staking his horse back on the trail. And it was dark. He thought he might see a campfire, but there was nothing. It was getting mighty cold at night; if Jethro was here, he was not put off by the cold.

He found a low hidden spot and waited patiently until morning. He did not stir a bone, scanning each possible spot for a bushwhacker to hide. He'd have to be in shooting distance of the crossing. He saw nothing.

By noon, he was ready to go back to fetch his horses. Then, he caught a movement in the brush. Carefully sighting with the Hawkins, he knew he'd not want to pull the trigger until he could clearly see what—or who—he was shooting.

Two riders with packhorses came up to the crossing from the south. Maybe this was what the bushwhacker had been waiting for! Dan knew he'd have to shoot a warning shot if the bushwhacker didn't show himself. And, sure enough, the riders were in the stream and still no sight of Jethro . . . if it was Jethro.

Finally, he could wait no longer and shot near to where he'd seen the movement. Before he could get the Hawkins reloaded, he saw a man stand and quickly disappear. A moment later, he saw Jethro moving fast upstream riding Max.

Dan walked down and met up with the travelers. They'd seen Jethro's quick departure and figured they'd been saved from being killed.

They'd talked to the man a day earlier and had gotten suspicious when the man was way too curious about what was on the packhorses.

Dan returned to his horse and rode back to the crossing where he picked up Jethro's trail. It was little help.

Dan followed the tracks into the river but could find no sign of tracks going out on the far side. Dan had hung onto one of the horses going over and dreaded a shot all the time from the bushwhacker. He moved slowly up the stream on the south side with no sign. Then he rode back down the stream. *Still no sign of tracks. Must have reversed in midstream and gone back to the north side. One smart bushwhacker,* Dan thought. *But I'm soaked and freezing, and I'm not going back across that river.*

The snow started coming down in large flakes.

He stopped, built a big fire, and got partially dried out. After drinking hot coffee, he was feeling more human. He headed off south and east trying to follow the ruts.

Days later, he reached Three Island Crossing, which he spent considerable time crossing. Heading east, he reached Fort Hall in deep snow.

The Fort was owned by the Hudson's Bay Company, and it had a vacant house since a clerk had died in late summer from cholera. Dan was made welcome—even though Americans were discouraged from immigrating to the Oregon Country. Instead, they were encouraged to migrate to California—and some did.

The Chief Factor was kind, and Dan spent a pleasant winter playing games with the half-breed boys at the fort and enjoying the meals cooked by the half-breed women. In return, he brought in much fresh meat to the fort.

He'd found no sign of Jethro.

Chapter 23

Spring

Dan lit out for Fort Boise in early spring. He'd not given up on Jethro, but a trapper who'd wintered at Fort Bridger had seen no sight of such a man. He had to have wintered westward, Dan concluded.

Again, he was coming up on Three Island Crossing going slowly west. He'd scouted the crossing for two days before making it over the river. Again, no Jethro. But it was a cold spring!

That evening, he settled down in a low spot—out of the cold wind—and fired up a blaze. The coffee was hot and good, and he was starting to feel human again. Then he got the shock of his life.

He sat stone still when the voice came from the darkness. "Well, hidy do, ole son."

His face turned white as snow, and his head was shaking from side to side.

Moss walked into the firelight and took a seat beside Dan. He reached down and poured coffee into his tin. Dan stared in absolute silence.

Looking at Moss's grinning face, Dan's wits slowly returned. He grinned and said, "Damn. You're sure hard to keep buried, Moss!"

They happily shook hands. Moss explained how he'd woken up in darkness and poked a hand up through the sod. He had managed to crawl out of the shallow hole he had been buried in.

"Dab it, Dan, you needs to larn burying. Put rocks atop a body! The damn wolves near got me!" Moss had gotten to the river and doctored his noggin, finding a big knot and a piece of badly torn scalp.

Dan related how he tried to stop the bleeding—and how Moss wasn't breathing.

"Well, not so's you could see, and that small heart were real quiet."

The old friends agreed it was lucky days in the end. Moss had wintered with an Indian tribe and "got fattened."

"I stayed at Fort Boise the winter before this last. I was ambushed west of the Snake that spring. This past winter I was up at Fort Hall. Had a run-in with Jethro at the Boise crossin'. But, he out-foxed me and got clean away."

"Dan, you and me's gotta start watching them river crossin's real careful, shore nuff!"

The old friends joined up, and took off in search of Jethro.

"Time to end his trail," said Moss.

Chapter 24

Fourth Winter

T he trail brought the trackers to two more remote
diggings where they stopped to pan for dust. They'd
done well but wasted much of the summer. There
had been no trace of Jethro. And the snows had come again.

It was the fourth winter since that long ago underground
darkness, Dan thought, and not yet on the way to the Columbia.
Then a bad thought came. *Was Colleen hitched to someone by now?*
Maybe he should give up on Jethro. He might even be dead!
He gave himself until the next summer to find a track or he'd
light out for Oregon Country.

They found an old cabin with three miners and were made
to feel at home. Best of all was finding an old friend.

"Well!" Jonathan said. "Ye be ne'er as tall as this son!"
This was overstating the truth, of course. But Dan had grown
since the wagon days. He was over six feet tall.

Moss and Dan traded meat for sleeping space in the old
cabin; it was pretty tight with five men sleeping on the dirt
floor. The fireplace was "fair to middlin'," as Moss said, and
they made do.

Dan took to carving animals with his old skinning knife
and furnished wood chips for the fire. One day, he was
whittling on a hunk of wood when Jonathan pulled out his

tattered Bible and began reading aloud. It was Christmas. Dan was startled to find warm feelings come into his chest. He had dim memory of the old times before Ma and Pa died. He and Sarah had been excited; they knew Pa had gone to the little town down the road earlier in the week. He'd surely have got a piece or two of hardtack sugar candy for Christmas.

It was a shock to remember that. How was Sarah? He wondered if she had little ones of her own.

He was startled to see Moss's face in the fire's glow. He had a faraway look and sparkling eyes. He never talked about his family or where he'd hailed from.

The day after Christmas was a tragic day at the cabin. Two of the miners were brothers. They had an argument that got heated; the younger brother killed the older brother with a hatchet.

Jonathan took over the proceedings. He called for a trial and appointed himself as judge. The guilty brother begged to be shot.

Jonathan said, "No. Has to be a trial!"

As there was nothing to say except he'd killed his brother, there was nothing left to say but what the penalty would be. They did not want to think about executing the man and shifted uncomfortably, not looking at one another.

Jonathan took up his Bible and said, "Well, this be a case a Cain and Abel boys. Best we banish him."

"What's that mean?" Moss asked, looking sick.

Dan wondered, too, how terrible that might be.

"It means he's to be turned out into the wilderness without hoss, provisions, or else."

That struck Dan as being a sort of death sentence as bad as shooting him—and maybe a whole lot worse in the snows of winter.

The guilty man asked if he could stay for the burying, and it was done.

Jonathan read his Good Book over the snow where the body was put, and the mourning brother walked off into the cold with only a shirt and no coat.

That evening, only three men slept in the cabin.

The next morning, Jonathan pulled out the old tattered cards and spread them on a rough plank before the fire. "We's got two pokes to draw high card on. Or do ye want to draw one poke to a time?"

They thought that drawing once for both pokes was most easy—and so it was done.

Each man pulled a card from the plank. Dan was high with a faint queen of hearts and pocketed the two pokes.

Jonathan laughed and said, "You're the winnin'est man I ever knowed!"

The brothers had no horses, but there was a small pile of their gear in the corner of the cabin. Moss won an old black powder single-shot pistol, and a good Hawkins rifle. That was all there was.

"Gotten to get some better pasteboards," Jonathan said. "Leastwise, we kin be closer to the fire nights!"

Chapter 25

Reflections and Search

D an was thinking more and more about chucking the chase. It was way past time to be off to Oregon, but he knew Moss would not turn back on getting Jethro. He, though, was torn between staying with Moss and heading west.

In the end, there was no choice. He couldn't let Moss go after the bushwhacker alone. As Pa had said, "Life ain't always fair. You just have to keep going on."

Dan reflected on the years since the wagons left. Mayhap, they didn't miss him much. It was a sobering thought. After all, he wasn't much. He still couldn't talk good and, likely, it was getting worse. And there was that question Colleen had posed. What did he plan to do with his life? He was still unsure.

He knew he'd not be a miner—though that had been good to him. Trapping had no attraction, for sure. He reflected that he was more and more like Moss . . . a wanderer.

He dreamt of what it was like in the Willamette Valley. Were Josh and Mary settled down on some cleared ground with planting done? Had Colleen waited for him? Why would she? He just wasn't much.

It was rough riding in the north Idaho country. Half the time, they were lost in tangled mountains.

Moss taught Dan to use the stars for navigating. "You never get total lost if'n you use the North Star and the Big Dipper and the Bear Stars. Daytime is when you get tangled up and turned around."

"Been thinking, Moss," Dan said. "Thinking what I'll do."

"What'er yer getting at, son?"

"Guess I'll turn my hand to running horses if'n I can. I mean, when I get to Oregon . . . breeding em, buying and selling."

"Sounds likely," Moss said, feeding wood to the fire.

"Suppose you might give it a try? Maybe we could go in together."

Moss was quiet for a long spell.

Dan thought he wasn't going to get any answer out of Moss.

When Dan was just closing his eyes, Moss said, "Yep. I'll give thought to it. Don't sound bad at all."

Chapter 26

Indians

As snow began to lower and buds were coming to the bushes, Dan and Moss neared the Tetons. They were on a high trail and spied a party of Indians riding hard on a small herd of buffalo. They'd watched and saw a buff fall to a small Indian in the lead. Something about it kept Dan's eye.

An idea popped into his head. He swung his horse down the long slope in a gallop. Moss followed close behind.

The Indians were quick to see the whites coming on and stopped in a group to watch. As they neared, the small Indian lit into a fast gallop toward the white men.

Sam and Dan shouted and grinned as they circled each other.

They ate buffalo hump that night while Dan and Sam renewed their friendship with tales of their doings. Dan explained how they were after Jethro.

Sam had to get back to the tribe, which was in dire need of meat. He had seen something that mystified him, but he was on the track of the buffalo and had moved on. They'd seen a white man near a river crossing, but there was no sign he'd ever crossed. The crossing was nearby. They were sure the white man had hunkered down somewhere near to the crossing. Maybe he'd spied Sam's band and laid low. It was a question.

In the morning, Sam said good-bye to Dan. He also stopped near Moss and said, "I know of you. You are Horned Owl. My people talk of you in our tepees."

Moss was mighty pleased and spoke in Shoshone, saying, "You people been good to me. Wintered with yer chief, Antelope, many winters ago."

Sam offered a rare honor; he reached out and shook hands with Dan's old friend.

Then, quick as lightning, they galloped away.

Chapter 27

Jethro

Dan told Moss about the white man at the crossing.

"Know's whar that be," Moss said. "Back some east a mite."

A few hours later, they caught sight of the river from a ridge. They talked about how to approach the crossing.

"If'n he's thar, reckon he's on the near side," Moss opined.

They figured and figured and, finally, decided on a dangerous plan. Dan wasn't happy but trusted Moss's judgment.

"All right, I'll do as you say. But you keep low and give me lots of time to get set."

Dan left his horse and got as near the crossing as possible, hiding among the higher rocks. He took extreme care to not be seen. He was about to conclude that no person was at the crossing when he spied horses hidden in the brush, and one was Max. "Oh! Be careful, Moss," he breathed. Dan looked and looked but couldn't see Jethro anywhere.

Moss was on the far side, getting set to cross.

Dan's forehead was dripping with sweat. Where was the varmint?

Moss was in the water, holding the saddle.

Throwing all caution to the wind, Dan stood to get a better sight of the boulders and brush below. When Dan was ready to yell a warning, he saw Jethro standing up to get a better sight on Moss.

Dan shot quickly. He saw dust come up square between the shoulders of the large man—and then he was gone from view. He hurried to set another ball on fresh power. In less than a minute, he was bounding down to where he'd last seen Jethro. The varmint was stone dead.

Moss met him and said, "The coyote gat his own medicines. Good riddance, you bet! An high time, too. Good shooting, Dan."

Dan was ready to return to Jethro's horses and gear. They walked to where Jethro had hidden Dan's old horse, Max, in a low spot with his mate, a packhorse. The large pack was on the grass near a cold campfire. Dan began sorting things from the pack while Moss was renewing his friendship with Max. There were several pokes—a right heavy load of gold. Dan said, "I'm guessing we's right comfortable gents with all this dust!"

One hand over the neck of Max, Moss waved a hand and said, "Naw! Gotten my riches all round me," He pointed at all the hills, snowcapped mountains, and Max.

Dan agreed; it was hard to find finer riches than the country around them.

He was looking for something he wanted more than the pokes and dug through the pack, tossing things into a pile. Near the bottom—and folded just as he'd last seen it—was the colored scarf.

Chapter 28

Homeward

They were drinking coffee near a small fire in the Blues when Dan happened to think of the rock he'd carried since his fall into the dark caravan. He pulled it from his possibles bag.

"Say, take a look-see at this rock." He tossed it to Moss.

Moss looked at it close and tossed it back. "That thar's a goldmine, son."

Dan stared at it for a while. Then he set it on a flat rock, and he smashed it with another rock. What emerged was a piece about the size of a walnut. He brushed it with a sleeve and saw why it was so heavy. It was a nugget. "I reckon I know where that goldmine is!"

They had fair weather through the Blues to the long, steep decline to the Columbia and down to The Dalles. There, they hitched to a wagon train. They began taking wheels off the wagons and setting the wagon beds onto rafts. It was hard work, and the water was rough most of the time. The horses and other livestock were loaded on separate rafts and taken down to the falls.

Dan and Moss were on rafts with horses—and not feeling good about any of it. It was a thing to raise your hair "quick as a Blackfoot," said Moss.

The big river was deep and swifter than any Moss or Dan had ever seen. It was downright scary, but they got to the falls and made shore without undue trouble. Mount Hood stood tall and proud on their left as they moved down the river, and they knew, once it was passed by, they'd be nearing the end of the long trek.

The gorge carved by the monstrous river was a wonder to both men. The cliffs rose high as they neared the falls. They walked around the falls with the horses and got back to the rafts below the falls.

Dan and Moss never wanted to see a raft again! When they pulled up at Fort Vancouver, Dan wondered how they might be received by the British. Moss was sure it'd be a treat.

They were as welcome as Dan had been at Fort Boise and Fort Hall. They ate like kings. McLaughlin was the chief but was gone on a trip to the north. Oh! To get potatoes and greens with salmon! It was good eating, and the two were nearly unable to walk when they left the long table.

"You knows how ter shovel the food," Moss said, but there was not an inch of fat on Dan's tall frame.

They looked over the big river and knew they had to cross the Columbia one more time.

Once they did—feeling good to be back on horses—they headed for Oregon City. They moved through thick forest and were dazed at the size of the timber. Some were eight feet and more in thickness.

They found Oregon City much to their liking—and saw the first stores they'd seen in years! Dan's hair was hanging below his shoulders, and he smelled mighty ripe. Baths and haircuts were a must.

Moss was for keeping his topnotch hanging long, but he consented to beard trimmings and a bath.

Dan and Moss were a big noise in Oregon City since they paid for things with dust.

Dan got the pokes turned in to a British agent and had a receipt in hand. He traded one poke for coins. He turned in cash for fair country wear and was clean and groomed into a tall gentleman.

Moss was keener on buying saddles and saddlebags. They went as men of wealth, trading old worn leather for new.

At the hardware store, they looked at new firearms. They held tightly to their Hawkins and left the new rifles in the store. They also found a place to bed down with a large room. And there was a large eating table down below. It was hard to stop eating potatoes, carrots, onions, berries, and fresh bread.

Dan had some shopping to do. He had no idea how to find his family, but he'd have plentiful gifts when he did. He remembered the wonderful treasure bag on the cottonwood. Moss was not a shopping man and waited patiently for Dan by finding a place to drink whiskey. He was ready to move on.

Dan finished shopping and found Moss sound asleep in their room. He was restless and wondered how he'd find his family. After thinking, he lit out for the livery barn and the horses. He found the man whose business it was and asked about Josh and Mary.

"Martin family? Mayhap, but you need to see Jackson o'er to the hardware store."

He'd met Jackson when they'd looked at the firearms and made his way back to the store.

Jackson scratched his head and thought but couldn't come up with anything that helped. "You might ought to stop down to Tualatin Plains and talk to Joe Meek. He knows a slew a folks."

He was about to take leave of the store when a settler touched him on the shoulder.

"Say, feller. Heard you ask about the Martins. Seemed to me I run into a feller by that name a few year ago. But not real shore. Thought it were down the valley not far from the Willamette River. But it be hard to know if that were the right people."

Dan talked with the man for a spell, but he couldn't be sure about much else.

Dan was walking through the door when the farmer said, "Mayhap they was a golden-haired girl thar?"

Dan stopped in his tracks. "Yes! That's the family! Josh, Mary, and Colleen!"

The man advised Dan to ride through French Prairie and follow the Willamette, checking with settlers along the way. He said that most settlers picked land near to folks they'd come with.

"I'd say to talk with Joe Meek like Jackson says. Joe does know a sight a folks."

Settlers were scattered throughout the long valley all the way to California.

Dan wondered if it was going to be a long hunt like it had been for Jethro.

Chapter 29

The Settlements

Moss was pleased with his new saddle gear, but he refused to trade his buckskin clothing for cotton. He did buy a wide-brim hat like Dan's new one.

They rode slowly south, stopping and talking to folks who were glad for new folks to talk with. A few roads were being run here and there, and the marks of civilization were appearing slowly. A settler told how they'd found some color at a place called Jacksonville.

They stuck together since it was unfamiliar territory; getting back after separating would be time consuming. They rode into the French Prairie and Champoeg settlements, but their inquiries brought nothing. When they rode into Tualatin Plains, it wasn't hard to find Joe Meek. Everyone knew him.

Joe was a good man, but his help was uncertain. He thought he'd met the Martins down the valley somewhere but couldn't be certain.

The days were passing, but Dan did not fret. He was ready to go at it as long as need be.

They went to both sides of the Willamette and found the Valley was a big, beautiful place. Dan came to love the Valley and knew it was home.

Land was being cleared, and stumps and limbs were being burned. Cabins were far apart for the most part, but folks were sure filling the upper valley. They rode south, crisscrossing the valley.

They pulled up to a cabin late in the day and lit for a talk with the settler and his wife. Invited to eat, they brought in some coffee.

The settler said, "Fust coffee we're seed in two year!"

They ate a thin, tasty potato stew.

The settler said, "No, couldn't rightly say I've heard of anyone by that name."

Dan changed the cotton clothes and learned to wash the ones that got muddied. *Moss is sure right about the buckskin*, he thought. Even wearing cotton, it was good to have clothes that fit again. He'd just grown, and grown, and outgrown his old buckskins.

Weeks went by, and it was early fall. They were about a mile from the Willamette when they rode up to a cabin. A man and a woman stood in the late day, looking out at their field.

Dan was stunned when Josh turned at the sound of the horses.

Mary turned too, but didn't appear to recognize him.

Josh stepped forward and said, "Light and rest yourselves. Where you from? Say, haven't we met afore?"

Moss grinned and said, "Mayhap, Josh!"

Josh looked close, and Mary quickly stepped up. She said, "Moss! It has been a long time!"

Moss was still grinning and said, "Shore have. We was west side a the Divide when I ate your biscuits, ma'am."

Mary laughed and stared at Dan. Her face went dead white, and she started to fall.

Dan grabbed her before she hit the ground.

"Daniel—"

Josh looked closely at Dan without saying a word. He stepped to Dan and hugged him and his wife together. "Son! In God's truth, we've prayed for this day!"

In the cabin, Mary couldn't stop her happy tears as she got Dan's coffee boiled and served.

Dan was sick that Colleen wasn't there. He was sure she was hitched to a settler somewhere.

Mary suddenly turned and said, "Dan! Sarah and Moses have come out and live just across the field!"

The door creaked open, and a girl stepped in. She looked up at Dan and froze. He smiled and pulled the colored scarf from his pocket. Suddenly tears sprang to her eyes and she was hugging him.

He was home.